There were jars of honey for sale, big cages of butterflies stacked together, baskets of different kinds of gems on the front counter, lilac and rosemary bushes on one side of the wall with bags of river rocks on the other. Tons of herbs, peppermint, licorice roots, berries, mushrooms, walnuts, tree bark, moss and rain water in jars were strewn about. Lightning bugs flew around near a sign on the wall saying, "One firefly per visit."

Keep your heart
young

Christina Cameron

House of Charms™

Pixie's Dust

written by
Christina Cameron

illustrated by
Randy Rasmussen

LOTUSME
PUBLISHING

© 2014 Christina Cameron
Illustrations by Randy Rasmussen

ISBN-10: 0-9908370-0-9
ISBN-13: 978-0-9908370-0-8

Printed in the United States of America.

Library of Congress Control Number: 2012916386

Dedicated

to my Nana Lillian A. Cameron

♦ ♦ ♦

A special thanks

to my family for all their help

Chapters

Chapter 1

Cedar Wood Way

The night was a strange one on Cedar Wood Way, a road with three cabins surrounded by thick forest. It usually got very dark and quiet at night, but now the sky was putting on a show as the rain fell hard, hitting the pavement like thundering applause, and angry bolts of lightning lit up the forest. A night like this was a treasure trove of inspiration for Pixie Elm, who at age 12 already knew she wanted to be a writer. Cedar Wood Way was home to three families in three log cabins. Each cabin had a second-floor balcony that looked out into the forest, and a patio circling around the bottom floor. The only detectable difference between each cabin was the uniquely carved front doors.

The three families on Cedar Wood Way each had one daughter, of exactly the same age. The Elm's owned the cabin in the middle, which had been in the family for many years. Pixie Elm was a pale girl with red hair; she had started writing for the school paper last year. Having the highest grade point average in school gave her the title of class bookworm, which she had no problem with. Writing was her passion; she didn't care if it gave her nerd status.

Sitting by her window looking out to the backyard on this dark rainy night, Pixie thought how fun it would be to feel the rain hitting her face as she ran through the forest, collecting raindrops on her tongue. A night like this was perfect for an adventurous mind like hers. One story she was working on was coming along beautifully, she thought. She would have to continue writing more in her journal, a beautiful green book that seemed to sparkle at night.

She had found this treasure at a yard sale with her mom, a woman who would travel the world for a good sale. The journal seemed to call out to her as she walked around the stranger's yard. She found it under a pile of old newspapers and books.

The woman selling her goods looked at Pixie with confusion, not recognizing the journal. "Oh, you can have that for free, darling; I've never seen that before in my life. Must have been here waiting for you to find," she said with a wink and a smile. Pixie thanked her and considered it a sign of good luck.

Looking around her room for a pencil and her flashlight, she spotted the journal on her desk, glowing green, inviting her to partake in some good storytelling. A night like this was perfect for coming up with some creative ideas. Pixie loved the ritual of setting up her journal and flashlight under the covers with her head forming a tent. While writing she would picture unknown places in her mind and the people she would meet there.

Pixie's gift for writing was inspired by Granny Josephine, who had lived with the family for many years until she passed away a few months ago. This was the saddest time ever in Pixie's life. She had spent many nights going back and forth with her granny about her stories. As Pixie looked at her journal, a tear fell at the thought of her beautiful and inspiring granny.

Every time the lightning flashed outside, Pixie could see through her blanket the green room surrounding her with everything she loved. She could see her beautiful matching white desk, her dresser and canopy bed, some books and notebooks that covered the desk along with her computer. She loved to keep lists to organize her life: school, career, travel and other things she needed. In a corner sat a small rocking chair from when she was a little girl. Now, her childhood bear from Granny Josephine, given to her when she was just two, is its owner.

On her wall was a blackboard with a list of books she would like to read. All of the great authors were on the list: Hemingway, Austen, and Bronte, to name a few.

Pixie only had one poster on her wall -- a collage of pictures from magazines, tickets from places she went, beautiful outdoor scenes, and in the center, a picture of Bob Dylan, a singer she was fond of, inspired by her parents' musical taste.

Another crack of thunder and Pixie looked out from under her blanket tentatively. As she got up with her flashlight to take a peek out the window, she noticed the big oak tree swaying oddly, almost like it was trying to tell her something. She opened her window to take a better look. At that moment, lightning struck the tree, causing a large branch to break away. The branch was lifted by a gust of wind and carried into the back woods. Pixie, startled, dropped her flashlight with a loud bang.

"Pixie, are you alright?" her mom called out. "What was that noise?"

"It's nothing, Mom. I'm fine."

"You better not be up writing all hours of the night. I think you should go to bed now."

"Alright, Mom. Good night."

"Good night, Pixie," said Mrs. Elm.

Pixie shut the window and got back into bed, putting her journal on her nightstand and thinking about the tree. The branch had seemed to fly on its own accord, she thought. Could she have just imagined it? Pixie wondered if her neighbors, Cinda and Tantra, had seen it too.

As her thoughts slowly drifted off, Pixie could hear the rain still beating down on Cedar Wood Way. The sound of the dog barking next door along with the soft thunder put Pixie into a deep sleep.

Little sparks of gold glitter started to hit Pixie's window like Fourth of July sparklers. But unfortunately, no one saw the sparks that night because everyone on Cedar Wood Way was fast asleep.

Chapter 2

The Elm Family Trunk

The next morning Pixie stretched as she slowly opened her eyes, trying to remember what she had seen the night before. Could it have been a dream? She had to check to be sure.

Pixie walked over to her window and took a peek at the tree. The large limb was gone and in its place was black soot on the trunk. "OK, so I'm not losing my mind; it did actually happen," she said out loud to herself.

The smells of bacon and eggs being cooked downstairs brought Pixie back to reality as she put on her bathrobe and headed downstairs to join her parents for breakfast.

Today the family planned on taking a bike ride through the woods. Mr. Elm loved the woods; he worked hard all summer one year to make a bike path for his family to enjoy together. The path started from the edge of the driveway on the side of the Birch family home and led to a stream with a peaceful open area, perfect for picnics. It was a two-mile ride that Pixie enjoyed taking at least once a week. Later that day they planned on going over to the Willow house to celebrate Mrs. Willow's birthday.

"Pixie, breakfast is ready," called Mrs. Elm.

Pixie headed into the kitchen and greeted her parents.

"Good morning, Pixie. I need you to help me with Mrs. Willow's gift later; I'm planning on a bundt cake-themed basket."

As Pixie sat down to eat, her dad looked up from his paper. "Hey, there's my girl all bright-eyed this morning," he said. "Were you able to get a good sleep last night with all that rain and thunder?"

"I loved it; it was the perfect inspiration for me to write more in my journal," said Pixie.

"I knew you were up writing late last night; what did I tell you about that? You need the proper amount of sleep," said Mrs. Elm.

"I was only up for an hour, Mom. I went to bed right after our tree in the backyard was hit with lightning. I watched a large branch break off and fly into the woods."

"What! Not the big oak tree in the backyard," said Mr. Elm.

"Oh, Pixie, I think you may have been dreaming. Look, Parker, the tree is fine," Mrs. Elm said to her husband.

"I really did see it, Mom. The tree swayed back and forth and then all of a sudden the large limb on the side broke off and landed in the woods."

Pixie's dad got up and looked through the kitchen window toward the oak tree, which looked fine. "I think you were dreaming, Pixie," said Mr. Elm.

Pixie walked over to the window. She also noticed the tree looked fine. How could it be? "I guess you're right. I must have been dreaming," she said. She decided the best thing to do was to agree with her parents, lest they think she was crazy.

As Pixie sat back down for breakfast her mom started talking about the bundt cake items she purchased for Mrs. Willow's birthday gift. The whole time her mom was talking, Pixie kept thinking about the tree. She felt the tree must have been trying to tell her something or lead her somewhere, but what or where?

"Pixie, have you been listening to what I've been saying?" her mother asked. "I need you to go up to the attic and find a basket that we can use for the gift."

"Sure, Mom, no problem." Pixie finished her breakfast and headed up the stairs toward the attic. She opened the door with the key hanging from a hook on the side of the wall. Inside the attic, Pixie was confronted with stacked boxes, books, baskets, old clothing, dolls and trinkets.

As she entered deeper into the room, Pixie noticed something odd in the corner that she had never seen before. It was an old dark wooden box that seemed to have something growing on it. It was almost hidden under boxes and blankets.

Pixie needed to get a closer look. But as she made her way through the boxes she tripped on some books on the floor. Her arms reached out to try to keep herself balanced, but she landed on some items on a dresser that fell to the floor. All she needed was her mom to come up and catch her being nosey before she could get a chance to check out the wooden box in the corner. She stayed still and the only thing she could hear was music coming from downstairs, the voice of Joni Mitchell. The coast was clear.

She approached the wooden box and saw that it was an old chest with moss growing on it. Pixie found a cloth on the floor and wiped away the dust and dirt covering the chest. She saw a brass-plated name tag below the lock that read, "Josephine Elm." Pixie thought it was odd that Granny Josephine's last name was Elm. Granny Josephine was her grandmother on her mother's side. Why was her last name Elm, the same as her dad's?

The lock on the trunk was very old; it needed a special key to open it. She searched around the attic trying to find the key with no luck. She felt like she was doing something she wasn't supposed to, but the trunk was her grandmother's; she needed to see what was in it. She continued looking around for the key until she heard footsteps coming up the stairs. After covering the trunk, she spotted a good basket for the gift and walked out just in time.

Her dad was coming up the stairs. She wanted to ask him about the trunk, but thought better of it and instead asked, "What do you think of this one?" as she held up a pretty braided basket.

"I think it's perfect; your mom will be happy," said her dad.

Pixie had a feeling that her dad had no idea about the trunk in the attic. She thought about asking her mom but decided it would be best if she tried to find the key first.

Pixie made her way downstairs with the basket to show her mom. "Hey, Mom, what do you think of this one?"

"It's perfect, Pixie. Thanks."

Pixie kissed her mom and headed upstairs to get dressed.

Mr. Elm went to the garage to get the bikes ready for their trip, while Mrs. Elm packed a light snack. Pixie loved spending time with her parents out in the woods, sitting on a blanket by the stream and looking up at the trees. It was so peaceful, a place to get away from it all.

The three headed out on the path with Mr. Elm leading the way. Pixie was in the back enjoying the view. When they made it to the stream, Pixie and her dad skipped stones while her mom looked on and prepared some cheese and crackers. The time went by quickly, as it always did when they were in the woods.

On the trip back, Pixie noticed something behind her house. As they turned the bend she could see it more clearly: a large tree branch that seemed like it had been struck by lightning, lying in the woods close to Pixie's backyard. She decided not to point it out to her parents.

It was getting close to one o'clock and the party next door was just getting started. Pixie and her parents walked over with the gift basket, and just as they were about to knock on the door Mrs. Willow opened it. "Happy Birthday," said Mrs. Elm as she held out the gift.

"Oh, thank you, Jill. I love your beautiful gift baskets; they're always so creative."

"Thanks, Dana. I was hoping you would like it," said Mrs. Elm.

"Please come in. Parker, you'll find my husband in the kitchen with the other men. Cinda is up in her room still getting ready, Pixie. Come on, Jill, I want you to meet some of my friends from work."

As Pixie looked around at all the guests, the Birches from next door were nowhere to be seen. Something had happened long ago that separated Tantra's family from Cinda and Pixie's that was never talked about. Pixie didn't know what it was, but one day she hoped to find out.

Pixie headed up the stairs to Cinda's room. As she entered the hallway she spotted Phooka, a black lab who adored Cinda, keeping watch in front of her room.

"Hey, Phooka, are you waiting for Cinda to get ready?" Pixie asked as she patted the dog on the head. As Phooka moaned a yes, Pixie could see Cinda in the mirror fixing her hair. Pixie had become good friends with Cinda Willow because they were neighbors, which was Pixie's only claim to fame in the popular crowd. Cinda was a thin, blond-haired girl, and on special occasions like this she liked to wear her hair up, always adding two pink barrettes whether it was up or down. Cinda loved parties; the whole idea of dressing up was exciting to her. She hoped to become a prima ballerina one day, and she had the stance of a dancer and the confidence of one too.

Cinda's family had moved to the United States from England less than a year ago, and in that time Cinda had made more friends than Pixie had made in her lifetime. Pixie had always been amazed in Cinda's talent to befriend everyone, but with Cinda being so kindhearted and friendly, who could resist her charm?

Cinda turned and invited Pixie in with her English accent. Everything in Cinda's room was pink: her bedspread, ballet shoes hanging on the wall, a big stuffed rabbit in the corner, plus pictures of pink flowers and dancers in pink outfits. No mistaking it, Cinda was definitely a girly-girl.

Phooka followed Pixie in, stretching as he slowly laid himself down on the multicolored pink rug in the center of the room, watching Cinda get ready. Phooka, who had been with the Willows since England, was a smart dog, sometimes showing human-like personality traits. He loved Cinda and would protect her if his life depended on it.

"Cinda, your mom seems very happy that everyone showed up for her party," Pixie said.

"Yes, Mum loves to have friends and family over whenever she can," said Cinda. "Come on, Pixie, let's join the party."

The house was now filled with people; trays of food were being passed around, with the sound of laughter and conversation flowing all through the house. There were so many people that the girls could walk out and no one would notice that they had left.

"Cinda, I want to talk to you about something I saw last night. Maybe we could go outside on the porch and talk," Pixie said.

"Sure, I just want to make my rounds first, and my mum has an announcement to make," said Cinda. "I'm not sure what it is, but she seemed excited about it."

Just then Mrs. Willow stood on the steps so everyone could hear her. "Everyone, I just want to thank you all for sharing this day with me, I'm very grateful to have wonderful people in my life. I want to tell you that I'll be taking a short trip to England to visit my homeland in Canterbury. I'm excited to see my friends and family over there again."

Cinda looked shocked. "I don't understand why she didn't tell me herself. I wonder if she is going alone."

"Do you think your dad knew about this trip?" asked Pixie. But as they watched Cinda's parents talking to everyone, it was obvious that Cinda's dad knew and he was excited about it.

"This is crazy. I don't know why they didn't tell me," said Cinda.

"There must be a reason," Pixie said. "I'm sure they will let you know more about it after the party."

"What did you want to talk to me about?" Cinda asked.

"Let's go outside. I want to show you something odd that I saw last night out my back window," Pixie said. She led the way to her backyard by the edge of the woods where she had spotted the branch.

"Last night I saw the oak tree in my backyard swaying and one of the limbs broke off, I think from lightning, but this morning when I looked at the tree it was fine. Then later this morning I saw this limb lying by the woods in my backyard. It's never been there before."

"Maybe your dad moved it there," Cinda said.

"No, he would have said something when I mentioned the tree this morning," Pixie replied.

"Your parents must think you're nuts, talking about a tree swaying and losing a limb, when obviously the tree is fine."

"They thought it was a dream, but I know what I saw. I think the tree was trying to tell me something last night, but I haven't been able to figure it out."

"Maybe it was trying to tell you to go back to bed."

"Very funny," said Pixie as she and Cinda looked at the branch lying at the edge of the forest.

Cinda started to walk on the large branch, leading her farther into the woods. As she got to the end of the limb, she noticed something stuck inside. "Hey, look at this; there is an old key stuck in this tree," Cinda said.

Pixie could hardly breathe when she heard Cinda mention a key. Could it be the key she needed to open the trunk? "Let me see it, I'm looking for a key to open my grandmother's trunk in the attic," she said.

"Do you think this could be the one? It looks real old," Cinda said.

"I'm not sure. I guess I'm just hoping it is." Pixie reached down and pulled the key out of the tree. It had the initials "J.E." printed on it. "Look, it *is* the key; the tree wanted me to find it so I could open the trunk. I think there might be something in there that I need to see."

"Does your mom know you want to open this trunk?" Cinda asked.

"Of course not, so please don't say anything about it. I'm not sure she wants anyone to know it exists. I need to do it now while my parents are still at your house. Can you call me when you see them leave to warn me that they're on their way home?"

"Sure, as long as you call me as soon as you find out what's in the trunk," said Cinda.

"Not a problem."

The girls parted and Pixie headed back to the house, key in hand and excited to finally be able to see what her grandmother had saved in that trunk.

Chapter 3

Map Through the Woods

How weird this all seemed, Pixie thought as she headed back to her house. How did the tree even know she would find her grandmother's trunk the day after the big storm, and why was the key outside in the woods? Pixie needed to find out what was going on; with the key to her grandmother's trunk she could finally see what her mom wanted to keep secret.

Pixie reached the house, opened the back door and headed straight for the attic. Making her way to the corner of the room where the trunk was hidden, she uncovered it to see if the key would fit. "I hope this works," she said to herself.

Pixie turned the key slowly, and the lock popped open with a jolt. Her hands began to shake with fear and excitement at what she might find inside. Lifting the top of the trunk, she saw many old and interesting things. There were books, sepia-toned photographs, news clippings, letters, a map, and a green dress with a small bag attached to it lying at the bottom of the chest.

Most of the books were some of the old classics Pixie remembered being read to by her grandmother. As she looked through the pictures, none of the people seemed familiar to her. Maybe they were family members way before her grandmother's time; by the looks of them, the pictures had to be pretty old. What caught Pixie's eye was the news clipping about a group of people living in the woods on a small commune. The article mentioned the names of some of the families that had lived together. The one's that stuck out were the Willows, the Elms and the Birches -- the same last names as herself, her friend Cinda Willow and Tantra Birch, her neighbor on the other side.

"This is crazy," Pixie thought. The article was from the late 1800s; it was hard to see the exact date. "Our families were friends back then?" It just didn't seem possible. She had to show Cinda the article. Pixie wanted to talk to Tantra about it too, but she would have to wait for the right time as Tantra didn't care for her much.

The letters turned out to be a bunch of old recipes that her grandmother had received from friends and family. Some of the recipes had ingredients like sticks, rocks, roots, flowers and other strange things.

As she reached into the chest again, Pixie pulled out an old map that seemed to have a trail leading deep into the woods. "Maybe it leads to the area of where the commune used to be." Pixie thought. By the looks of it the trail led to a shack deep into the woods. There was a name written on the map, but it was hard to decipher; some of the writing had faded away. Pixie decided to take the map and the newspaper article out of the chest and keep them in her room.

Looking deep into the chest, Pixie reached in and took out the old green dress. She touched the see-through

15

bag attached and felt a sand-like substance inside it; it was green -- a color that Pixie was fond of. An odd coincidence, Pixie thought.

She decided to leave the dress in the chest, thinking it may be risky having the dress in her room where her mom could easily find it.

As Pixie put the remaining books and pictures back into the chest, she heard the phone ring and remembered that Cinda was supposed to call her if her parents were on their way back home. Pixie locked the chest quickly and covered it up the way she had found it. Leaving the attic in a hurry with the map and article clutched tightly in her arms, she dashed to her room to hide the papers inside her backpack.

Pixie reached over just in time to answer the phone. "Hello," she said.

"Hi, this is Tip Top Pro Care services. You could win a trip to Hawaii today! Are your parents home?" asked the excited voice on the other end.

"Sorry, sir, we're not interested," Pixie said. She hung up the phone and retrieved her backpack, putting the key deep inside her desk drawer before she made her way back to the Willow house to show Cinda what she had found.

On her way back to Cinda's she glanced out to the backyard and noticed that the limb where they had found the key inside was gone. That was weird, but then everything seemed odd to her now. As she made her way to Cinda's front door she noticed that more people had arrived since she left; this made it easy for her to make it back in without being seen. She walked in and searched for Cinda.

Pixie spotted her parents talking with friends in the kitchen. As she carefully passed by, she ran into

Cinda talking to her grandfather in the hallway. "Hey, Granddad Willow, it's nice to see you," Pixie said.

"Hello, Pixie. What are you two girls up to these days? I sense something is up. You can tell me, you know; I can keep secrets pretty well."

"Granddad, nothing is going on, just girl stuff. School is starting soon so we want to be prepared," Pixie said.

"Alright, but when you need a wise ear you two know where to get it." He smiled at them and walked toward the kitchen where Pixie's parents greeted him.

"That was odd," said Pixie.

"Yes, quite," said Cinda as she stared at her granddad. "So did the key open the trunk?" asked Cinda.

"Yes, it did. You have to see some of the things I found," Pixie replied.

"Bring it upstairs to my room so our parents don't catch us talking about it," Cinda said. Phooka lead the way back up the stairs, seemingly curious himself.

As they got to Cinda's room they sat on the bed while Pixie pulled out the article and the map from her backpack. "Take a look at this article; it talks about a commune of people living together in the woods," she said.

As Cinda read the article and looked at the pictures, she noticed the last names of some of the families and her face became pale. "How could this be? Did our families really know each other way back then?" asked Cinda.

"I was as surprised as you are when I read the article; the date is hard to make out but it definitely is from the late 1800s."

"How weird that your grandmother would have saved something like this. It must have some meaning that binds our families together. The other names don't look familiar to me, though," Cinda said as she handed the article back to Pixie.

"I don't recognize the names either, but they must have been good friends to live together in a commune," Pixie said. "I also found this map in the trunk; it looks like it leads deep into the woods to a shack."

Cinda looked at the map with surprise and excitement. "Wow, a real old-fashioned treasure map."

"I'm not sure the house is a treasure, but it would be fun to try to find out where it is," Pixie said.

"Oh, Pixie, this could be a treasure to your grandmother."

"Yeah, I guess you're right. I think we should try to find this house."

As the girls studied the map, Pixie noticed something familiar on it, a place that she and her family had been many times. "I think I have been to this part that looks like a stream," she said. "It looks like the one we rode our bikes to just this morning."

"What are you saying?" asked Cinda.

"I know how to get to the stream that leads to the house in the woods," said Pixie.

Pixie looked at Cinda and they both shared in the excitement of a new adventure. Just then there was a knock on the door and Pixie's mom peeked in.

"Oh, there you girls are. We're getting ready to leave now, Pixie. School starts tomorrow so I think it would be a good idea to get to bed early tonight."

"I'll be right down, Mom," Pixie said.

"Ok, I'll meet you downstairs."

Pixie got up and put the papers into her backpack. "Maybe we can plan a trip out to the house soon," said Pixie.

"I'm not sure that's a good idea; it looks pretty deep in the woods. From the looks of it, we could get lost," Cinda said.

"Well, I'm planning on going to find the treasure. I think you'll be missing out on a great adventure."

"I'll have to think about it. See you tomorrow morning at the bus stop."

"Ok, I'll see you then." Pixie headed down the stairs as Phooka barked a goodbye.

The party had cleared out quite a bit; Pixie's parents and a few other couples were the only ones left. "It was a great party, Mrs. Willow. Happy Birthday!" said Pixie as she hugged her on her way out with her parents.

As Pixie's parents stepped off the porch with their good-byes, Cinda's granddad caught Pixie's arm and whispered to her, "Remember what I said; just give me a call if you girls need anything answered."

"Ok, I will, Granddad Willow," said Pixie.

On her walk home with her family all Pixie could think about was the map through the woods and the strange comment Cinda's granddad had made. It was like he knew what they were talking about, but Pixie dismissed this. How could he know about their discovery?

Later that night Pixie's dreams led her to a small, unusual house deep in the woods. She felt like she was visiting a familiar place, one she knew all too well.

Chapter 4

Skater Girl

Pixie woke to the sound of birds chirping outside her back window and the smell of coffee brewing downstairs. It was the first day back to school and the air had the slight chill of a September morning with a crispy white frost covering the grass. Pixie liked school, but she wasn't fond of getting up so early; she had no choice if she wanted to catch the bus.

Her thoughts were still on the map as she got dressed in jeans and a cute top and headed for the kitchen.

"Good morning on this cold crisp day, my lady. Would you like some oatmeal?" asked her dad.

"Sure, that sounds good," Pixie said.

"Are you ready for another school year?" her dad asked.

"Yes, I'm ready as I'll ever be," Pixie said. "The school newspaper meeting will probably be sometime this week; I can't wait to see my friends and start writing again."

"My little writer, don't forget your harp lessons after school," said Mr. Elm.

"That's right; Mr. Bloom will be here at 4:30 so don't be late for the lesson, Pixie," added Mrs. Elm.

As her parents continued to get ready for work, Pixie headed for the bus stop. Pixie's dad worked as an accountant at a firm and her mom worked at a florist shop a few days during the week.

The bus stop was right in front of Tantra's driveway. Cinda and Pixie liked to meet earlier so they had time to talk, mostly about boys or what they had planned for the week, because when they got to school they usually went their separate ways. Even though they hung out in different crowds they still talked.

Cinda, decked out in a pretty pink dress and carrying a cute purse, walked briskly to the bus stop, excited to start the first day of school. Pixie, with her backpack, usually dressed more casual for school. While the girls waited together and talked about the first day they heard the Birch's front door open.

Out came Tantra, dressed in black ripped shorts to the knee, a black and white T-shirt, short socks, and her favorite black sneakers with purple laces in them. Her hair was black, cut spiky short, and her eyes were outlined black -- a typical Tantra look. A messenger bag was draped over her body. She skateboarded down a ramp she had made off the side of her front steps. "Hey, losers. What are you two talking about?" she asked.

"Hello to you, too," said Pixie.

"Whatever," said Tantra, giving Pixie a look and skating around to avoid talking to them.

Just then the bus could be seen coming up the hill to Cedar Wood Way. Tantra cut in front of Pixie and Cinda as the doors opened, making her way to the back of the bus where some of her friends were sitting. Pixie and Cinda took a seat together closer to the front. The bus was small since Cedar Wood Way had hardly any houses on it. Most of the kids who went to Cedar Middle School lived in the town of Cedar, about three miles away.

On the ride to school Pixie turned to Cinda and whispered, "I want to talk to Tantra about what I found since her family name is also in the article."

"Good luck with that. In case you haven't noticed she doesn't like us that much," Cinda said.

"Yeah, I've noticed, but maybe this will break the ice; who knows, maybe it could lead to a new friendship."

"Whatever you say, Pixie."

"I'm thinking about trying to follow that map through the woods sometime this week. I want to try to find that house," Pixie said. "Are you sure you're not interested?"

"Oh, come on, Pixie. Do you really think that place still exists after all these years? And besides that, you only know where the beginning of the trail leads; how are you going to find your way through the woods without getting lost?"

"Maybe if I had some help with the map we could try to figure it out together."

"I'm not sure I want to take part in this search. Sometimes things are just better left undone," Cinda said.

"I can't believe you're not interested in finding out what all this means," Pixie said. "It has to do with our families; it could be something important."

"I'm a little nervous about the whole deep in the woods thing," Cinda said.

"We could take a few days at a time to work on the map, to see how far the trail goes."

"Ok, Pixie. Maybe I'll start out in the beginning of this search but I still don't think I'm ready for the whole adventure."

"That's fine, Cinda. Maybe we could bring Phooka to help us with the trail."

"I'm sure he would love to go; he loves the woods," said Cinda.

"Great, then it's a plan. We'll meet tomorrow after school at the starting point of the map, which is exactly where my dad started the bike trail."

As the bus edged its way to school, Tantra and her friends made their way to the front of the bus. As soon as the doors opened, they jumped on their boards and skated to the school, vanishing before Pixie and Cinda made it off the bus.

"Cinda, I wanted to ask you about your mom. Did she leave for England yet?"

"She's getting ready to leave soon. My mum is excited about the trip. All I know is that she plans on visiting some of her friends, but I feel like there is more to it than that."

As the girls got closer to the school, Cinda's friends spotted her and called her over.

"I'll see you later after school," said Pixie.

"Ok," said Cinda, joining the girls.

Pixie was left alone looking for her homeroom and really wanting to investigate the map and figure out the directions on it. She walked by a group of people all dressed like Tantra. Pixie spotted Tantra among them and felt the urge to talk to her, but thought better of it when she caught Tantra whispering and laughing with one of her friends while pointing at her as she walked by.

Pixie finally found her homeroom, where everyone was already seated and talking, excited about the first day of school. Pixie took a seat toward the front when she noticed her good friend Carl walk in.

"Hey Pixie, great to see you," Carl said. "I just found out that the school paper will be starting this Friday. I can't wait to get started on it again."

"I can't wait either. I miss everyone, especially the feeling when we all get together and brainstorm some great ideas," said Pixie.

"I know what you mean. It's going to be great this year since it's our final year in middle school. We definitely will take charge of most of the articles."

As Pixie and Carl continued to talk, the school bully, Joel, walked in and took a seat behind Pixie, joining his friends. "Look at what we have here, Miss Know-It-All ready to start another year of showing everyone up."

Joel and his friends laughed as Pixie turned around in her seat. "Is that all you got, Joel? I think you need to work on your put-down skills; they're not working."

Joel gave Pixie a dirty look. She was one of his main targets. Pixie hated it until she finally found it in herself to give it right back. She hated to do it, but it seemed to work.

The homeroom bell rang and everyone took their seats for the morning announcements. After the announcements there was a loud commotion of students going in different directions to their first classes.

Pixie's first class was biology, right down the hall from her homeroom. She took a seat at the lab table close to the front by the windows. The class started to fill up and Pixie noticed a handsome boy with long blond hair walk in. She didn't recognize him, so figured he was new. He sat down next to her with a smile.

"Hi, my name is Zeb. I just moved here from California," he said.

"Hi, Zeb, I'm Pixie. What made your family move to New York?"

"Most of my family are from around here; my parents just wanted to be closer to everyone, so here I am. It seems a lot different than California, though."

"I'm sure it is," Pixie said.

"I'm good at adjusting to new things, so I'm looking at it as an adventure," Zeb said.

Pixie laughed. She noticed that Zeb seemed to like skateboarding since his binder had skate stickers all over it. He would probably find his way into the skater group.

A short, dark-haired woman wearing a white lab coat walked in and took a seat at the head of the class behind the lab desk. She seemed to be the same size as most of the students, making it hard to find her when she walked around.

"Alright, class, please be quiet. My name is Mrs. Stevens," she said. "Just to inform you, you might as well get to know the person next to you since this will be your lab partner for the rest of the year."

"Hey, it looks like you're stuck with me. I hope that's OK," said Zeb.

"I think I can deal with it," said Pixie with a smile.

Mrs. Stevens handed out the lab assignments for the following week. "Class, this is how it works," she said. "We will have lectures Mondays, Wednesdays and Fridays; quizzes will fall on every second Friday. Tuesdays and Thursdays you will be working on your lab assignments with your partner. There will be ten tests during the course of the year, plus each lab will count as a quiz, so make sure you and your partner are working together."

School had just started and already it seemed like the homework was piling up, thought Pixie. The biology lecture seemed to go on forever when finally the bell rang, jolting Pixie out of her daze.

"Well, Pixie, until we meet again. Enjoy the rest of your day," said Zeb.

"Thanks, Zeb, I will. Who knows, maybe we will run into each other again sometime today."

"Yes, you never know."

Zeb waved and took off down the hall where he met up with some of the skater crowd. He must have met them during the summer at the skating park, Pixie thought. It crossed her mind while walking to her next class that knowing Zeb might be the perfect way to get to know Tantra. Pixie really wanted to show her the old article about their families knowing each other all these years and, of course, about the map to the house in the woods. She hoped she could talk both Cinda and Tantra into going with her to find it. That was a long shot, but she was feeling good about things lately.

As Pixie made her way through her classes, she collected tons of homework that she hoped she had time for now that she had a new adventure in her life. Her next class was English, one of her favorites. Pixie walked into the room and saw her teacher, Mrs. Peters, a thin, stylishly dressed woman who wore her blond hair twisted up in the back. Pixie had heard great things about her teaching style. She took a seat in the front row, excited to start class until Joel walked in and sat down next to her.

"Joel, are you sitting here just to bother me?" Pixie asked.

"Now, come on, give me more credit than that. I'm here to learn just like you," Joel said with a smirk.

"Hi, everyone. I'm Mrs. Peters and this is English/Writing class. I like to add 'writing' because most of our assignments will deal with the writing of short stories."

"You must be getting all warm and fuzzy inside; this is right up your alley," said Joel to Pixie.

"So, first off, I would like everyone to have a journal going that I will check once a month. Pick a journal that will inspire your writing."

"How lame is this. Why do we need to write in a stupid journal? It sounds like a waste of time. Live life, why go back and write about it," said Joel. Pixie rolled her eyes, hoping he would be quiet.

"First off, it's a great way to be creative in your thinking, and second it's because I said so, so get a journal," said Mrs. Peters, giving Joel a sarcastic smile. She then passed out the syllabus for the class. Pixie was excited; to put words on paper and share them with others was a dream come true for her.

"This is what I would like everyone to do for homework for the week: Pick an object from your home and write something about it that would be interesting to share with the class," said Mrs. Peters. "Also, finish chapter one in your books and answer the questions at the end."

"Hey, Pixie, where are you heading to now?" asked Carl as he caught up to her in the hall after class.

"It looks like I have lunch right now. What about you?"

"Me too; do you want to head in together?"

"Sure that would be great," Pixie said. It was always easier to go to lunch on the first day with someone she knew. "I think Molly and Jane have lunch now; maybe we can try to find them." Pixie spotted the girls as they entered the lunchroom and headed over to their table with Carl.

"Hi, you two; how are things going? Are you getting ready to start the paper this year?" asked Pixie.

"We can't wait. We were just discussing some great ideas for this year. We wanted to run them by you to see what you think since you'll be heading it again," said Molly to Pixie.

The group talked more about the paper as Cinda entered the cafeteria with her friends; following was Tantra and the skater crowd. Pixie noticed Zeb walking in with Tantra's group and he looked in her direction.

"Pixie, nice to see you again. It's been awhile; how are things since science class?" asked Zeb. Molly and Jane stared at Zeb as if he was a Greek god, while Carl rolled his eyes.

"I'm fine so far. Tons of homework, though, but that goes with the territory."

"Yeah, I hear you there," Zeb said.

Tantra turned to see whom Zeb was talking to and noticed it was Pixie. A look of disgust came across her face as she made her way over to Zeb. "What are you doing? We don't associate with this group; they're book nerds if you haven't noticed."

"I'm talking to a new friend. What's wrong with that?"

"Whatever, do what you wish." With that Tantra turned and walked away with her friends.

"Well, that was rude. Sorry about that," said Zeb.

"That's ok, I'm used to it. Tantra doesn't care for me too much. We're neighbors," Pixie said.

"She seems nice once you get to know her. I guess that will be one of my goals this year, to get the two of you together to become friends."

"That would be cool," said Pixie.

"I'll work on it. I guess I'll see you around. Bye, Pixie."

"Bye, Zeb."

"Ok, who was that and how did you meet him?" asked Jane.

"That was Zeb. He moved here from California. He's my lab partner and, yes, I know he's hot."

"I don't see it. You girls have no taste sometimes," said Carl.

"Someone sounds jealous," said Molly.

"Oh, please. I'm above being jealous of some other guy, especially one from California." Carl got up and walked to the lunch line.

"Wow, what was that about?" asked Jane.

"I can answer that," said Molly. "Carl has a crush on Pixie that has been going on since last year."

"We're just friends. He doesn't like me like that. You're crazy," Pixie said.

"Whatever you say, Pixie. It's so obvious though," said Molly.

"I hope not, because I don't like Carl that way. I'd hate to hurt his feelings," Pixie said before Carl returned with his lunch.

Pixie noticed Cinda sitting with her friends at an opposite table and waved. Cinda waved to her as she got up from her group and walked over to Pixie. "How are things going so far with your classes?" asked Cinda.

"My teachers seem to be nice but they sure like to give a lot of homework," Pixie replied. "I can't believe we haven't been in the same class yet."

"I know; I was thinking the same thing," said Cinda.

"I only have woodworking, study hall and gym left; all my major classes were before lunch," Pixie said, showing Cinda her schedule.

"We have gym together at least," said Cinda. "We can talk about Tantra then."

"Has she been in any of your classes?" asked Pixie.

"Yes, and I got a chance to talk to her. She mentioned something that I thought you should know, but I'll tell you later."

"Thanks, leave me in suspense," Pixie said. Cinda got up and waved to Pixie as she rejoined her friends.

"Now, Cinda. That girl is hot," said Carl, looking down at his food. Pixie and the girls looked at him and laughed in a friendly way.

The bell rang and Pixie said goodbye to her friends as she headed for her woodworking class. She didn't know the first thing about woodworking, but she figured she was about to find out. Pixie noticed there were just a few girls in the class. Pixie was just about to join them when she noticed Tantra and Zeb walk in and take seats at the front.

"Hey, Pixie. Come join us," said Zeb.

"It's nice seeing you again in another class," said Pixie.

"Imagine, three times today. How can I be so lucky?" asked Zeb.

"Hello, everyone. I'm Mr. Zack, the woodworking genius," said the teacher. "No, just kidding, well, yes I am. No, ha ha. Yes. Oh, no." Mr. Zack was a little odd in an eccentric way. While he talked he walked back and forth as if he was trying to figure out what would be the right thing to say. "Ok, yes, right, here we are ready to venture into the craft of woodworking, the fun we will have. Oh, yes, ha, ha the fun."

Everyone looked at one another, not sure what to make of Mr. Zack. "Alright everyone, I'm going to pass out some graph paper. I want you to imagine something that you would like to make and then draw it the best you can. Don't worry if it's not coming out right; it's all in the process of creating. No rushing, now. I want to see some creative ideas." Mr. Zack was dancing around while passing out the papers. Everyone was quiet at first but as soon as Mr. Zack danced his way to his workbench the chatter began about how odd he was and what were they going to make.

"He's great, don't you think?" asked Zeb, starting his sketch.

"Yeah, very entertaining," said Tantra.

"I think it will be an interesting class, but I'm not sure what I would like to make," said Pixie, staring at her graph paper.

"I want to make a skate ramp, but I don't think that will fly, so I think I'll make a bench," said Zeb.

"I'm thinking about making a jewelry box with a secret drawer inside," said Tantra.

Pixie thought about her grandmother's trunk and the map. She wanted to talk to Tantra about it but still felt the timing was not right. She would have to wait till later. Maybe Cinda has already talked to her, she thought. As she continued to think about the map, Pixie's hand started drawing something on her paper; she looked down and watched herself draw a beautiful picture of a birdhouse. "I guess I'm going to make a birdhouse," said Pixie in disbelief.

"Hey, that's great. You're good at drawing," said Zeb.

"Thanks. I honestly don't know how I did it. Drawing is not something that comes naturally to me."

The bell rang as Pixie handed Mr. Zack her birdhouse sketch. Mr. Zack stared at Pixie's drawing with a look of shock. He looked up at Pixie. "This is a butterfly house. It's beautiful. I haven't seen one of these in years. How did you know how to draw one?" he asked.

"I thought it was a birdhouse. I didn't know butterflies had houses," Pixie said.

"Some do, some do," said Mr. Zack as he walked away, lost in his thoughts.

"That was odd," said Zeb to Pixie.

"Yeah, I was thinking the same thing."

"While you two lovebirds talk about nonsense, I'm out of here. See you later, Zeb," said Tantra.

"Yeah, I'm on my way out too. Bye, Pixie," said Zeb.

"Bye, Zeb."

Pixie made her way down the hall to the auditorium for study hall. She worked on her math homework while thinking about the strange butterfly house that Mr. Zack looked startled by. She had almost felt like someone else was using her hand to draw it. It was strange. Just as she finished her last math problem the bell rang.

Pixie couldn't wait to get to gym class, where she could talk to Cinda about her conversation with Tantra. It was a mystery to Pixie how Cinda seemed to be able to talk to everyone. Pixie wanted to know how Cinda was able to get anything out of Tantra without her walking away.

The gym was way down at the other end of the school, so Pixie had to pick up her pace to make it in time to change for class. As she entered the locker room everyone seemed to be dressed and ready to go. She hurried out of her clothes and caught up to the other girls who were walking into the gym. Pixie saw Cinda talking to a group of girls by the volleyball net, while Tantra was hanging out with her two good friends Samantha and Avery on the other side.

"Hey, Pixie, over here," called Molly, who was hanging out with Cinda's group.

"Oh, Pixie, over here," said Samantha in a sarcastic voice, while Tantra and Avery laughed. As Pixie headed over to Molly, Ms. Webb entered the gym, wearing a whistle around her neck and carrying a volleyball in her left hand and a clipboard under her arm. She was a physically fit woman standing 6 feet tall with short, blond curly hair. She looked like she meant business.

"Alright, girls. No one is skating by in my gym class, so working hard is going to get you somewhere in here. I expect everyone to jog five laps around the gym before the class starts. I have eyes in the back of my head, so I'll know if someone is not doing their laps. Don't get on my bad side; it's not a good thing." Everyone seemed to take what she said seriously. Ms. Webb blew the whistle and shouted, "OK, FIVE LAPS NOW. GET A MOVE ON!"

All the girls took off in a jog around the gym while Ms. Webb called out their names. "Avery Adams."

"Here!"

"Tantra Birch."

"Here!"

"Carole Bonini"

"Here!"

Pixie was glad she had been active over the summer, because she felt that she could make it around five times no problem, but she could see some of the other girls were having a harder time and she felt their pain.

"Come on, we don't have all day, girls. This is only a 45-minute class," Ms. Webb said.

Pixie finished fourth behind Tantra, Cinda and Avery. Samantha was right behind Pixie, with the other nine girls slowly making their way to the end. "Alright, well, that was pathetic; it looks like we have our work cut out for us," Ms. Webb said. "The two girls finishing first and second will be captains and will pick their teams for the volleyball match."

Tantra and Cinda headed up toward Ms. Webb. Tantra picked her friends Samantha and Avery, along with Keely and Kendal, who were twins, plus Beth and Max. Cinda picked Carole, her best friend, Pixie, Molly, Trina, Rain and Marie. The girls set out on the court, with Tantra and Samantha hitting the ball hard, mostly trying to knock the others down.

"Hey, easy with the volley. We don't want anyone getting hurt," said Ms. Webb.

"What fun is that?" Samantha said to Tantra as they laughed. Every time a volley would start either Tantra, Samantha or Avery would try to aim at Pixie's head. Pixie had fast reflexes, though, and was able to hit it back or to her teammates. Tantra's team seemed to be a little better at their returns, which helped them win the game.

"Yeah, we won, we're the better team," said Tantra.

"Ok, that's enough. It's not about who won, it's about how you play the game, so be good sports and go over and shake hands," said Ms. Webb.

The girls made a line and hit hands with a "good game" added in.

"Alright, that's it for today, but next class we will talk about the game of volleyball, so taking notes would be a good idea."

"Gee, that's crazy, notes in gym class," Tantra said, rolling her eyes.

"Don't question my ways, just follow them. Now get dressed," said Ms. Webb. The girls left the gym to change.

"Hey, Pixie, wait up. How was the first day for you? Everything you thought it would be?" asked Molly.

"It wasn't that bad. I like my teachers. I have Mr. Zack for woodworking, he seems a little odd, though."

"I heard about him; he likes to dance and sing around the class," Molly said.

"Yup, that's him," said Pixie.

Pixie threw her gym clothes into her backpack , and as Pixie and Molly turned the corner out of the gym they bumped straight into Tantra, Samantha and Avery.

"Hey, how does it feel to be a couple of losers?" asked Tantra.

"Oh, good one; that definitely hurts. How about you, Molly, are you hurting?" asked Pixie.

"Yeah, big time," said Molly.

"You gals are so funny. I wish I could be just like you," said Tantra, pointing at Pixie while Samantha and Avery laughed.

"Come on, Pixie, let's just head out. I don't like associating with mean people," said Molly, leading the way out of the locker room.

"Mean people? Mean people? She doesn't like mean people. Who's being mean?" asked Avery. Tantra and her friends began to laugh as the bell rang to end the first day of school.

Everyone piled out in a rush in search of their buses, while Pixie looked around trying to find Cinda. She spotted her talking to Carole and some other girls.

"I'll see you tomorrow, Pixie," said Molly as she headed toward her bus.

"Yes, we'll talk about the newspaper tomorrow. See you." Pixie waved good-bye as she headed over to Cinda.

"Hi, Pixie. We were just talking about a new boy in school. He's so hot," said Carole.

"Does he have long blond hair, about 6 feet tall and just moved here from California?" asked Pixie.

"Yes that's him. Have you met him?"

"He's my lab partner in biology and he's also in my woodworking class," Pixie said.

"What's he like?" asked Cinda.

"He's really nice. The only thing is he hangs out with Tantra and her skater friends," Pixie said.

"That figures. Maybe he will come to his senses," said Carole.

The girls said good-bye to one another as Pixie followed Cinda to the bus. Taking a seat, Pixie said, "The suspense is killing me; what did Tantra tell you? And, by the way, how did you get her to talk to you in a civilized manner?"

"I wanted to talk to you earlier, but I didn't think Tantra would end up in our gym class," Cinda said.

"I know. How much fun was that?"

"First off she seems to be OK with me," Cinda said. "I just approached her and asked her if she has ever been in the back woods by the stream."

"You asked her that? What did she say?"

"She said she had, and she mentioned finding some weird prints on some of the trees farther down from the stream," Cinda said.

"Do you think that might lead to the house in the woods?" Pixie asked.

"I don't know, but it sounded like something you might be interested in."

"Thanks. I wonder how far Tantra followed the marks," said Pixie.

"I'm not sure, but I think if she had found some house she may not have mentioned the markings on the trees."

"That's true; she wouldn't want us to find something that she found."

"I agree," said Cinda.

"I've been in those woods so many times; I don't remember ever seeing marks on the trees."

"Maybe you weren't looking high enough in the trees; Tantra said the marks are pretty high up."

"It must be the trail. We have to go tomorrow after school," said Pixie.

"I'll go, but maybe not all the way," Cinda said. "We shouldn't stay in the woods too long; it does get dark there at night."

The bus opened at the girls' stop. Pixie and Cinda jumped off and said their good-byes as they headed to their houses. Cinda had to get ready for ballet practice and Pixie had a harp lesson. Pixie opened her front door to the sound of her harp being played by Mr. Bloom, who always arrived early. He was a nervous, short, heavyset man who liked to walk around with his hands on the top of his head while Pixie played her harp.

"Pixie, is that you?"

"Yes, Mom. I just got off the bus."

"Great. Mr. Bloom is here already, so why don't you start the lesson early."

"Sure, let me just drop my books up in my room and I'll be right down."

Pixie got herself ready for her harp lesson and headed down the stairs. "So, Pixie, have you been practicing the piece we worked on last week?" asked Mr. Bloom.

"Yes, I have. I love the way the notes seem to form in that piece."

"Great, then let's get started."

Mr. Bloom proceeded to walk around the room with his hands on his head, listening to Pixie play. "That's good, don't rush it now, even motion, feel the piece," he said. Pixie continued playing while she lost herself in the music. Suddenly her hands started playing something

37

she never heard before, something different. Where it was coming from she didn't know. She felt like she was in a trance. Just then a dish crashed on the floor in the kitchen where her mom was making dinner. Pixie, startled by the sound, came to her senses just in time to see Mr. Bloom standing next to her shaking before he ran out the front door.

Chapter 5

House of Charms

Mr. Elm was walking up his driveway when the front door flew open and he saw Mr. Bloom rushing out of the house. "Hey, Mr. Bloom, how did the harp lesson go today?" he asked.

"Oh, just fine. Have to go, though, have to go."

Mr. Elm watched the harp teacher run to his car. He appeared to be quite pale and a bit flustered. What had his daughter done to cause this poor man to be in such a state?

Mr. Elm opened his front door. "Hello, I'm home. Anything happen that I should know about?"

Pixie was in the kitchen with her mom helping her clean up the broken glass. "We're in here, Dad," called Pixie.

"What's going on here? I pulled in the driveway and almost got plowed down by Mr. Bloom."

"I'm not sure what happened. I think it was something I was playing on the harp that startled him. Do you know, Mom?" Pixie asked.

"You know how Mr. Bloom gets when he hears music," Mrs. Elm said. "It's like he loses himself in it. I think he just got excited about Pixie's progress and left before the lesson was over without realizing it ."

"I don't know, Mom. He looked kind of shocked at something I was playing, and you also must have been, too; you never break plates."

"This is crazy talk, Pixie. Why don't you start your homework before we eat," said Mrs. Elm.

Pixie left the kitchen and headed up to her room to start her homework, but before she did she wanted to write about all the weird things that were happening to her since she opened that trunk of her grandmother's. She definitely needed to follow the map into the woods; maybe then she could figure out what was going on. There had to be something she needed to find out. Why did it seem like this place on the map was calling to her?

Later, as the family had dinner mostly in silence, Mr. Elm spoke up: "Pixie, I think I would like to hear this new piece of music since it caused such a stir earlier. My daughter is now writing her own music."

"I don't know if I can play it again, Dad. I'm not sure how I played it in the first place. My hands seemed to move without me doing it."

Mrs. Elm began to cough after taking a drink of water and couldn't stop.

"Honey, are you ok?" asked Mr. Elm.

"I'm fine, Parker. I think that we should forget about the song and let Pixie work on the music she is supposed to learn."

"That's fine, but I would like to hear a little of the song. Maybe she has a talent for creating music that we don't know about."

"I'll try to play it again," said Pixie as she got up from the table to sit by the harp. She tried to play the piece that her fingers seemed to know all too well, but after three failed attempts she realized she couldn't remember it. "Sorry, Dad. I don't think I can remember any of it now," she said.

"That's OK. It takes time to acquire those skills. I'm sure it will come back to you," said her dad.

"Well, that's that. Let's get this kitchen cleared so we can have some time to relax," said Pixie's mom.

Later, after her homework was completed, Pixie's thoughts were on her walk with Cinda through the woods tomorrow after school to follow the clues in the trees. She had a feeling that this would all lead to the house in the woods.

While Pixie was thinking about the trip, her mom and dad walked into her room to say goodnight. "Dream good thoughts, Pixie," said her dad.

"Goodnight, see you tomorrow," said Pixie. The lights went out and all she could think about was that house that might still exist deep in the woods, and it filled her dreams with pleasant thoughts.

The next morning Pixie hurried to get ready for school, but her real desire was getting home afterward to start the adventure. Her parents were already up having breakfast when Pixie headed downstairs.

"You seem to be excited about school today; I didn't even have to get you up this morning," said Mrs. Elm.

"I can't wait to see my friends from the paper so we can start coming up with ideas," Pixie lied.

"Is Carl still working on the school paper too? I like that boy," said Mr. Elm.

"Yes, he will be working on the paper again this year," Pixie replied. I'm happy that the group I started working with is still going to be in the club."

"Well, have fun with it. Enjoy these years, Pixie; they go by so fast," said Mr. Elm.

"I will, Dad." Pixie got up, said goodbye to her parents and headed out for the bus with her heavy backpack, excited to talk to Cinda about their plans after school.

Pixie was alone outside for a while. She felt like she had been waiting forever until Cinda finally joined her about a half hour later.

"Hey, Pixie, you're out here early. What's up with you?" Cinda asked. "Did you enjoy your first day of school so much that you can't wait to go back?"

"Very funny, Cinda. I'm just looking forward to our trip to the woods after school; I guess I can't wait to start this day."

"How do you think we can make it out there without our parents wondering what we're up to?" Cinda asked.

Pixie hadn't thought about that part, but it would definitely be an issue if they didn't make it home in time for dinner. "I think our only option is to lie to our parents so we can start our adventure right after school." Pixie said.

"What are we going to say? I'm not really into lying to my family," said Cinda.

"It's not a big lie. We'll tell them that we need to work on a school project together and we need to start it right after school, so we may be late for dinner. This gives us time to follow the map."

"I guess that would work, but what if they ask us what we're working on?"

Pixie thought about this for a bit. "It's a biology assignment that we each have to work on, collecting things from outside," she said.

"I guess that might work. I still don't feel right about it, though," Cinda said. "Maybe we should tell our parents what we found; they might be interested in seeing if the map does still lead to a house. They might even be able to tell us about the article you found about our families living in the woods."

"No, we can't mention this to anyone. I really think my mom wants to keep it a secret for some reason."

"Pixie, maybe your mom is right; we should just leave it alone."

"My grandmother saved these things for a reason," Pixie said. "I feel I need to do this for her."

"Alright, you talked me into it."

As the bus approached the driveway Tantra skated out of her house, making it just in time. She took a seat in the back of the bus.

"Where should we meet after telling our parents about this make-believe biology assignment?" asked Cinda.

"We'll meet in my backyard and then take the trail to the stream. From there we can follow the map the rest of the way."

"I'll bring Phooka with me. He loves the woods," said Cinda.

"Great, maybe he could help us with the trail," Pixie said.

The girls continued to talk as the bus approached school. "Have fun in your classes, Pixie!" Cinda said as she jumped off to join her friends, while Tantra pushed Pixie out of the way, smiling as she walked by.

"Bye, Pixie," Tantra said as her friends followed her out, laughing.

"Bye, Tantra," said Pixie in a similarly mocking voice, rolling her eyes.

Nothing could bother Pixie today. Her mind was on getting the day finished so she could get back home to find the house in the woods.

Pixie walked into homeroom and noticed Joel doing something to her chair. As she got closer she found tape stuck to a piece of paper on her chair; after she sat down she would have had some silly note stuck to her backside. Pixie reached down and picked up the note. Joel and his friends looked disappointed that she had found it. Pixie read the note: "Kick me." She turned to Joel and said, "Now that's original. How did you possibly come up with that one all by yourself?" Joel gave Pixie a dirty look and turned around to talk to his friends.

Pixie sat across from Carl, who was busy doing last-minute homework. "I was going to remove the note from your chair but Joel said he'd beat me up and I'm not really into that sort of thing. I was planning on telling you about it before you stood up, though," he said.

"Thanks for looking out for me," Pixie said. "It's fine. I know Joel can be a jerk sometimes."

After the school announcements, Carl and Pixie talked about their ideas for the paper. "I think this year we should interview different students to find out their interests and concerns about school," said Carl.

"That sounds like a great idea," Pixie said. "We should probably talk to Mrs. Thorn to help get us started on it as soon as possible. Maybe we can meet with her sometime before the club starts."

The bell rang and Pixie and Carl walked out of homeroom together. "See you at lunch, Pixie."

"I'll see you then."

Pixie walked into her biology class and her assigned lab table. Zeb walked in looking just as good as he did yesterday, in a happy mood and smiling at Pixie. "Hey, partner, are you ready to rock this lab out of the park?"

"Sure, whatever you say, Zeb."

"Alright, everyone. On your desk you will find today's assignment," Mrs. Stevens said as she closed the door. "We will start this class with a nature lesson since we are into fall, a great time of the year, don't you agree? I would like you to collect some leaves from different kinds of trees when you get home. Five different leaves and the names of the trees they come from would be great. Bring them in and I will iron them in wax paper so they will preserve. Five leaves only per lab group. Not that hard, I suspect."

Pixie couldn't believe her luck. She and Cinda wouldn't have to lie to their parents at all; she really did have a biology assignment right after school. An assignment that had to be completed in the woods. What are the odds of that, she thought. "I can collect the leaves when I get home; my house is surrounded by trees," Pixie said to Zeb.

"That would be great 'cause I have plans at the skater park after school. I want to get in as much skating as I can before this snow I keep hearing about happens."

"No problem," said Pixie.

The first assignment was about how plants capture the sun's energy and store it during photosynthesis. Pixie had read the chapter yesterday so she had some idea of how this worked. She started to draw a leaf and its layers while Zeb wrote out the formula and the photosynthesis process. Pixie was surprised how detailed Zeb was with the assignment; he was even more particular than she would be. She was happy he took the class assignments as seriously as she did.

Mrs. Stevens collected the lab work before the bell rang and said, "Don't forget your outdoor assignment for tomorrow."

Later in math class Pixie couldn't help but watch the clock. She couldn't wait to get home already; she had a map to follow. After the bell finally rang, Pixie was off again.

She made it through art and history class and it seemed like the day was actually going to fly by until she stepped into her English class. Pixie noticed that the desks were in a circle. She took a seat with the other students in the circle and Mrs. Peters handed out sheets of paper with instructions.

"OK, class. Today we are going to work in groups of two. I have a bag with numbers in it to pair everyone up. If you have the same number as someone else, that is your partner for this assignment."

The assignment was to interview your partner and write a short paragraph about them to share with the class. "This is going to be fun; don't look so excited now," said Mrs. Peters as she passed the bag around so everyone could get a number. There were twenty-six students in class, making thirteen pairs. Pixie reached in the bag and pulled out a piece of paper with the number thirteen on it.

As everyone searched for their partners, Joel strolled into class late. "Hello, Mr. Emerson, you're late for class," said Mrs. Peters.

"I know, I know," said Joel.

"Please take the last number. That number will be your partner for today's assignment."

Pixie was starting to worry; everyone else seemed to be pairing up. That could only mean … "I've got lucky thirteen." shouted Joel. Who has thirteen?"

Pixie wanted to run out the door and never look back, but instead she said, "It looks like we're partners today," and gave Joel a standoffish look.

"I guess thirteen isn't always lucky," he said.

"I guess not," said Pixie.

"This should be fun," said Joel, looking bored as he took a seat next to Pixie. "What are we doing?"

"We have to write a paragraph about each other and then present it to the class. We have ten minutes to talk and ten minutes to write and then we have to present it."

"Are you kidding? This is a nightmare; am I having a bad dream right now? Please someone wake me," said Joel. Some of the students laughed.

"Ok, that's enough, Joel," said Mrs. Peters, "Everyone start your interviews. I'll be timing them."

"What should I know about you besides that you're a complete jerk?" asked Pixie.

"Well, if you must know I'm on the football team. Quarterback. Sure to get the girls that way."

Pixie rolled her eyes.

"I like hot cars, cool bikes and warm food. Favorite subject: gym, then lunch. I plan to be rich and famous someday." Pixie jotted everything down while Joel talked about himself.

"Do you want to ask me anything? We only have ten minutes," said Pixie.

"No, I know all I need to know about you; you're easy to figure out."

"Class, your ten minutes are up," said Mrs. Peters. "Start writing for ten minutes now."

Pixie began writing, trying to make Joel sound somewhat decent. She really could make him look stupid right now, but she knew that would disappoint Mrs. Peters. She wanted to make a good impression in her favorite class. Pixie looked over at Joel as he wrote something down and started laughing. Great, he's going to humiliate me, she thought.

"Alright, class, let's get started on those introductions," said Mrs. Peters.

A girl named Ann stood up. She wore a pretty dress and matching shoes; her hair was perfectly in place. Pixie recognized her as one of Cinda's friends. "Kelly loves to sing; she is in the chorus here at school. She sings to her three cats that she loves so much; their names are ..." Ann kept talking, trying to look cute while Kelly giggled next to her. "Class, this is Kelly Johnson." Ann pointed to Kelly as she sat down to applause. Joel rolled his eyes.

The interviews continued like this one by one. Pixie kept her eye on the clock, hoping the class would end soon.

"We're getting to our last group. I think we may have just enough time," said Mrs. Peters.

Pixie looked at Joel and decided she should start since he made no effort to get up. "Hi, my name is Pixie and I had the opportunity to interview Joel and get a brief glance at some of his favorite things," she said. "He loves autumn time -- its when football season starts and now that he has made first string quarterback for our football team he finds more pleasure in the game by playing the field." A few students laughed at that comment. "His favorite interests are cars and bikes, and he likes all types of food. He wants to make a difference in the world, to be recognized for his achievements. Class, this is Joel Emerson."

Everyone clapped as Joel looked at Pixie oddly, trying to figure her out. He slowly stood up. "Hey, this is Joel. I interviewed Pixie she's a ..."

Just then the bell rang and Mrs. Peters piped up. "Joel, we will start tomorrow's class with your introduction. Everyone, please don't forget to get an idea of an object in your house you would like to write about to share with the class. Great interviews, everyone," Mrs. Peters shouted as the class headed out. Pixie was relieved.

As Joel watched Pixie leave, he wanted to thank her for what she had said but decided against it when he saw two of his friends approaching. When he walked out of class, his paper fell to the floor and Mrs. Peters picked it up and read the paragraph he had written about Pixie. Shaking her head, she folded the paper up and put it in her purse.

Pixie made her way to lunch, where her friends Molly, Jane and Carl were waiting. "Hey, Pixie. I talked to Mrs. Thorn, and our newspaper club will be starting this Friday," said Carl.

"All the clubs will be starting then; sign-ups are tomorrow. I hope we get a good group of people interested in it this year," added Molly.

"That would be great. What other clubs do they have this year?" asked Pixie.

"I've heard they added the art club, debate club and the book club, and they're keeping the sports club, chess club and biology club," said Jane.

On Friday mornings the clubs met before the regular classes, which were shortened by five minutes. If a student didn't want to participate in a club they had to sit in a study hall instead. Most kids picked a club.

Pixie and her friends headed to the lunch line to get their food and then made their way to an open table. As her friends talked about clubs, Pixie started to daydream about her and Cinda's trip to the woods in search of the house on the map. She couldn't wait; only three more classes until it was time to head home.

"What's the matter, Pixie? You look like you're somewhere else right now," asked Carl.

"Oh, I'm fine. Just thinking about English class, my homework, stuff like that," answered Pixie as the bell finally rang.

Woodworking class went smoothly, and Tantra didn't bother Pixie at all. Mr. Zack passed back everyone's assignment from the day before. He added comments on what changes needed to be made and how to make them, using a smiley face as a period at the end of each sentence. Pixie looked around and noticed that most of the students had quite a few red marks on their papers. Her paper only had a few suggestions with a few more smiley faces on it.

As the class was coming to an end Mr. Zack went around collecting papers, singing and dancing. Approaching Pixie, Mr. Zack whispered in her ear, "I can't wait to see your finished project, Pixie," and continued dancing around the class.

"Mr. Zack seems to really like your idea about this butterfly house," said Zeb after class.

"I know. It's kind of freaking me out a little. I'm not sure what I'm doing but it seems to be right."

"You're doing well, Pixie. Concentrate on that."

"Thanks, Zeb. I guess I'll see you tomorrow."

"For sure." Zeb took off down the hall and waved back at Pixie.

Pixie survived study hall and was now making her way to her last class a bit late, getting her gym clothes on while everyone else was already running their five laps.

Pixie finally entered the gym to join the other girls, and she was startled as Ms. Webb shouted, "Well it's about time, Miss Elm. Make that six laps around the gym." Tantra and her friends giggled as they passed Pixie. She had to figure out a different way to get to the gym or else she would continue to be late. The other girls finished their laps, heading to the bleachers to take a seat while Pixie finished hers.

That day's volleyball game seemed to be more intense, with each side trying to dominate the other. "Good work, girls. That's how a volleyball game is played," "That's a wrap." said Ms. Webb.

Pixie didn't get a chance to speak to Cinda during class because of the intense game that ended in a tie.

Once Pixie made it out of school, she headed for her bus. She anticipated meeting up with Cinda, but she couldn't find her anywhere in the mass of people leaving school so decided to wait for her on the bus.

As Pixie looked out the window she spotted Cinda saying goodbye to her friends, turning in a fast walk to hop on the bus. "Hey, Pixie, you'll never guess what."

"Let me guess, you have a science project that may lead you into the woods in search of leaves so you won't have to lie to your parents?" Pixie asked.

"How did you know?" asked Cinda.

"I have to collect leaves for a science project so I was hoping you would too."

"I'm so happy I don't have to make up some story. My mum is leaving for England tomorrow so I don't want to stay out too late," Cinda said.

"That's fine. I just can't wait to get started. I was thinking we could meet by the oak tree in my backyard, collect our leaves, and then follow the map."

"That sounds perfect; I just don't want to stay out past dark. If we don't find this place today we'll have to do it some other time," said Cinda. Pixie said she understood.

The bus stopped in front of the girls' houses and they ran to tell their parents about the science project that would send them out to the woods and cause them to miss dinner.

Pixie waited by the oak tree with her backpack filled with the map, a camera, a flashlight and her journal, just in case she had a chance to write about her findings.

Cinda was running late by nearly half an hour, wasting valuable time, Pixie thought. Finally Cinda's door opened and she jumped out, running toward Pixie in a cute pink jacket with matching jeans and pink and white sneakers. She carried a bag, Phooka following behind.

"Sorry I'm late," she said. "My dad made us sandwiches and I had to wait till he was done or he would have made me stay for dinner. I know you wouldn't be happy with that," said Cinda, out of breath. Pixie thought Cinda's tardiness probably had more to do with her changing into a different outfit, but decided not to mention it.

"That's fine; let's get going."

They collected their leaves on the way into the woods, following the trail with Phooka in the lead. When they reached the stream Pixie opened up her backpack and pulled out her journal while Cinda placed the leaves between the pages. Pixie then took out the map and the flashlight since the forest was making it dark.

"It looks like we need to continue to follow the path until it crosses the stream," said Pixie. Cinda took the sandwiches out of her bag and handed one to Pixie while taking one herself and giving Phooka a dog treat. Pixie held the map while Cinda carried the flashlight, lighting the way where Phooka was happily leading, wagging his tail. The girls made their way through the woods to the part where the trail bent to the right onto a wooden bridge leading to the other side of the stream and then back on the path made by Pixie's dad on the other side.

"This must be where Tantra saw the marks on the trees but I don't see anything; do you?" asked Pixie.

Cinda looked around while following Phooka across the bridge. "Pixie, look. I think I found it," she suddenly said.

Cinda shined the flashlight up at a tree with some kind of symbol or picture on it. The girls took a closer look at the marking. "That looks like a butterfly or butterfly wings," said Pixie.

"It does. Look, there are more," Cinda said, shining the light on the trees.

The girls got excited as they walked faster, following the strange markings deeper into the woods. They both stopped when they came to an odd clearing of dead brush. It was a large area in the shape of a circle. The circle looked kind of depressing, as if something bad had happened there. There were no signs of life, and nothing seemed to be growing in the area.

As Pixie held up the map, the girls tried to find their location. "I think we may be at this spot where it looks like a cluster of plants used to be," said Pixie. The girls followed Phooka as he walked through the circle.

"I feel something. I'm not sure what it is, but it's like I'm happy to be here. I feel alive," said Cinda as she held out her arms and propelled herself around the circle, laughing. Pixie was starting to feel it too. She ran around in circles with her hands raised high, looking up at the sky and feeling the early night air on her face. Phooka followed them around until he smelled something on the other side of the circle and started barking as he trotted to the wooded area. Cinda and Pixie followed Phooka deeper in the woods, laughing as they jumped over tree

53

limbs and walked over large rocks across a running stream. The girls kept a steady pace, trying to keep up with Phooka, still feeling strangely calm and comfortable in this environment.

Phooka suddenly stopped in front of a group of boulders so high that the girls could hide behind them. The dog slowly moved to the side of one of the boulders, lying on the ground and staring at something.

"Pixie, I'm scared. Where are we?" Cinda asked. "It's dark now; what happens if we're lost?"

Pixie was scared too, but she didn't want Cinda to know. Instead she moved along the boulder to see what Phooka was looking at. As she slowly turned around the side of the boulder she spotted something.

It couldn't be. Not after all these years, she thought. "Hey, Cinda, come here and look at this."

Cinda slowly moved over to where Pixie and Phooka were and peeked around the boulder, seeing the old shack. "It can't be," said Cinda.

"Look, lights are on inside and there seems to be a sign hanging on top of the door," said Pixie. The girls tried to make out what the sign said but the shack was a little ways up and surrounded by trees and brush.

"Pixie, go up there and see what it says," said Cinda, clinging to the boulder nervously. Pixie was afraid to go, but she was the one who had persuaded Cinda to take this trip in the first place.

Pixie slowly made her way closer, trying not to be seen, then reached a spot where she could read the sign. She whispered to Cinda, "It says the House of Charms."

Pixie and Cinda checked the map and saw the same name: House of Charms. They looked at each other in shock as an old voice from the house yelled out, "Is someone there?"

Chapter 6

Midnight Plans
and Quarter Moons

The girls hid behind the boulder, trying hard not to make a sound, both unsure what their next move should be. Then, without warning, Phooka leapt out behind the boulder and started barking at the old woman. The girls tried to get Phooka to stop, but to no avail. He seemed to have a plan of his own.

The old woman shouted, "Who's there?"

Phooka made his way toward the light of the front porch so she could take a look at him. He sat down and started whimpering. Then, finally getting his courage up, he trotted over to the porch so she could pet him.

"Well, hello there. You look like you could use a treat; let me see what I have." The old woman went into the house and returned with a licorice root. "Oh yes, how about this?" Phooka gladly took the root in his mouth, trotting around like he had received a prized ribbon. He then took a slow, happy walk back toward the woods where he disappeared into the darkness, and the old woman closed the door.

The girls were both nervous as they crawled back into the woods in the hopes of finding Phooka to help get them home safely. Holding hands, they called out for him as quietly as they could. "Phooka, Phooka where are you? We need you. Please, Phooka," called Cinda.

Suddenly something hit the back of Pixie's leg and she let out a screech. She jumped and turned around to see Phooka sniffing at her pant leg.

"Phooka, you scared us. We thought we lost you. Help us find our way out of here; it's getting dark," said Cinda.

Pixie checked her watch and saw it was only six thirty -- earlier then she thought but darker then she had hoped. Phooka took his instructions right after be buried the licorice root and covered it up with dirt. He let out a bark and headed back out of the woods the way they came.

"I guess that was the house we were looking for," said Pixie. "Cinda, doesn't this increase your curiosity about what it means or who that woman was? Aren't you curious now?" asked Pixie.

"I don't know; I can only think that the house has been there for many years and a poor old woman found it and decided to live there."

"Cinda, how can you think that? Don't you want to find out what the House of Charms is?"

"I'm not sure I really want to know. That woman seemed to want her privacy. I think we should leave her alone."

"But this house is a part of our past. I think it would be important for us to know more. My grandmother saved these things for a reason."

Cinda kept walking slowly behind Phooka, looking down and thinking about what Pixie had said. "I'm just scared," Cinda said. "What happens if it's something we shouldn't know about, or maybe our parents do know but don't want it to resurface? I think it's a secret that should be kept quiet. Obviously your mum knows about the items in the trunk and she didn't tell you anything about it."

"Yes, but that doesn't make it right. I really think my grandmother wanted us to have this information and find out what it all means," Pixie said.

The girls finally made it out of the woods and back on the bike trail, which led them out toward the road on the side of Tantra's house. "I think I'm going to tell Tantra about what we found. She should know, too, since her family also is a part of it," said Pixie.

"Good luck with that. She will probably think you're crazy and won't believe anything you have to say."

"That may be true, but I have to include her. She may be interested in a weird sort of way," Pixie said.

"Do what you have to, but I'm not sure I want to continue on this adventure."

As they stopped in Pixie's backyard, Pixie opened her backpack and handed Cinda her five leaves. "I hope you change your mind," she said. "I was hoping you would do this with me."

"I need to think about it first. I don't want to rush into some mysterious caper just yet."

"Suit yourself. See you tomorrow."

"Yeah, see you tomorrow," said Cinda as she headed toward her house.

Pixie opened the back door to the kitchen and flew up the stairs toward her room, but her mom stopped her midway. "Where are you running to in such a hurry, young lady? Don't you think you should have something to eat first before sprinting upstairs?"

"Sure, Mom. I just want to drop my backpack off. I'll be right down."

"Ok, dear. Did you find what you were looking for?" asked Pixie's mom.

Pixie froze in the hallway and turned to face her mom on the stairs. "What did you say?" she asked, sounding guilty.

"Did you get the leaves for your project?"

"Oh, yes, we both did. It was easy; there were so many different trees around it was hard to pick which ones we wanted."

Pixie headed downstairs and had a bowl of soup. As she was eating she tried to think of ways to talk to Tantra. She had no idea how she would be able to get her to listen. Maybe school wasn't the right place to tell her.

She finally decided to go over to Tantra's house after school tomorrow. Satisfied, Pixie put her bowl in the sink and sprinted up the stairs to start her homework. All her thoughts now were on Tantra. How was she going to approach her, and would Tantra even bother to listen? A good night's sleep would do her well, she thought. She needed all the help she could get.

Lying in bed, Pixie reached for her flashlight and journal and began to write about the House of Charms. At the end she wrote: "Cinda, Tantra and I come from a different line of people; we come from something special." Placing her journal on the floor, Pixie settled back in bed where she drifted off and had odd dreams: visions of a fire and people running or flying away, she wasn't sure which. Whatever was happening, it was bad.

Waking up early for school, Pixie still felt sleepy after a rough night of bad dreams. She couldn't wait for the day to end, which was unlike her since she really did like school.

Waiting at the bus stop alone made Pixie think how badly she wanted to go back to bed. The bus approached and Pixie forced herself up the steps and took a seat close to the front. Cinda and Tantra both made it just in time before the bus took off.

"When are you planning on telling Tantra about this House of Charms?" asked Cinda in a low voice.

"I'm thinking it might be best if I wait until after school. Maybe I can go over to her house and talk to her then," Pixie said.

"She usually goes to the skate park after school; you might be able to catch her there."

"Yeah, right, she probably will be hanging out with her friends. The last thing she wants to see is me showing up to talk about something like that," said Pixie.

"I guess you're right. Well, good luck with that," Cinda said. "I don't see her being interested in something we found in the woods, especially if it ties our families together. Can't you just hear her now?"

"Yes," said Pixie. "You're right; she probably won't care."

As the bus pulled up in front of the school, the girls jumped off and joined the rest of their classmates. Tantra skated past the two of them to find her friends. Pixie wanted more than anything for Cinda and Tantra to be interested in exploring with her.

Just then Pixie remembered that today Joel would be reading his paper about her to the class. She started to feel anxious about what he might say. I can't let him get to me; it will only make him happy, she thought.

Pixie headed to homeroom and ran into Carl. "Hey, Pixie, we can sign up for our club classes today in homeroom," he said.

"That's the one thing I'm looking forward to today," said Pixie.

Mr. Sycamore, Pixie's homeroom teacher, had the activities listed on the board, and the students took turns signing up for the club they wanted to join. When Pixie made it up to the list, she noticed that the sports club and art club were the most popular in her homeroom. Carl and Pixie were the only ones signed up for the newspaper.

As the day went on, the dreaded English class approached. Pixie wasn't looking forward to it but she had to get it over with sooner or later. Joel wasn't in homeroom that morning, making Pixie feel somewhat relieved that maybe he wouldn't show up for English, either. Unfortunately, as soon as she entered class there he was sitting up front in a discussion with Mrs. Peters.

The class piled in as Mrs. Peters spoke: "Class, we need to hear one more interview before we get on with the next topic of our writing assignments. Joel, will you be so kind as to read your interview to the class, please."

Joel stood up, turning around to look at the class as he read his paper. "Hi, class. My name is Joel and I had the opportunity to interview Pixie yesterday. She loves to write, which is why she gets involved in our school newspaper. Most of her writing is very inspiring and creative, especially the interview section she does with students about topics on things we care about. Not many people know this, but Pixie has a talent for playing the harp that has been passed down in her family from generation to generation. Class, I would like you to meet Pixie Elm."

The class clapped as Joel sat back down. Pixie couldn't believe her ears; did he really write those nice things about her? Was that really Joel or was he warned by Mrs. Peters to say something nice? How did Joel know about her harp playing? She didn't think anyone knew except some of her closest friends.

As class came to an end Pixie wanted to thank Joel, but before she could he was already out the door. I guess I should just be happy, Pixie thought. I don't want to push a good thing.

As Pixie entered her woodworking class she noticed Zeb and the other students picking out wood for their projects. "Hey, Pixie," Zeb said. "I forgot to tell you in science class: I decided to sign up for the newspaper club. I thought it would be a fun way to get to know more people."

"That's so stupid," Tantra piped up. "Why would you want to know anyone else? You're already associated with the best people in school. The newspaper club is littered with a bunch of whiny nobodies."

"Thanks, Tantra. I always considered myself that, but I didn't think anyone noticed," Pixie shot back.

"OK, you two. I think we should all try to be friends. I've gotten to know you both separately and I think the two of you would make great friends if you gave it a chance," said Zeb, stepping between them.

"I can't see that happening," said Tantra, while Pixie rolled her eyes. The three worked in silence on their projects till it was time to leave.

Zeb walked up to Pixie after class. "She is nice, you know," he said. "I think the two of you would make great friends."

"Like she said, I don't see it happening anytime soon," said Pixie. "I'm glad you're joining the newspaper club; it is a lot of fun despite what Tantra says."

"I'm looking forward to it," said Zeb. "I'll see you later."

As Pixie entered the auditorium early for study hall she noticed her homeroom teacher, Mr. Sycamore, opening a door under the stage and disappearing behind it. How odd, she thought, that she had never noticed that door before. She decided to take a look.

Walking up to it slowly, she twisted the knob and it opened with a creak. She saw a flight of stairs going down under the school. It looked like a secret passageway, Pixie thought. Slowly stepping down the stairs, she kept her ears open in case Mr. Sycamore was close by. At the bottom of the stairs was a cave-like tunnel that seemed to extend the entire length of the school. Pixie started to walk down the hallway when she heard voices ahead. She crouched down and listened. It sounded like Mr. Sycamore was talking to Mrs. Thorn, Pixie's history teacher and head of the newspaper. They were talking about some strange things that had been happening to them lately. Then their voices trailed away and Pixie heard a door close in the distance.

As Pixie made her way further down the hall it became darker and darker; she guided herself by feeling along the walls. She finally found stairs that led out of the dark passageway to a door up top. As she opened the door she found herself in a closet filled with piles of old papers, brooms, buckets, deflated basketballs, cones and someone's swim trunks. The closet had a swinging door that opened to another door. Through that was the main hallway where Pixie found herself right in front of her gym class. She waited for the bell to ring before entering the hall to the gym; the last thing she wanted was to get caught now that she found this secret treasure. Pixie was happy that she now had a way to get from study hall to her gym class on time.

Cinda approached Pixie in the locker room. "I was thinking last night about you wanting to tell Tantra about what we found. Why don't we talk to her after gym?" she said. "Maybe if we both talk to her she might be interested."

"That would be great, but I think it would work best if you were the one talking since she seems to like you more than me," said Pixie.

"It's a plan." The girls separated and started their five laps.

After gym class, Pixie and Cinda waited to catch Tantra before she took off with her skater friends. It was awhile before she finally exited the gym with her skateboard in hand. Pixie and Cinda picked up the pace and walked along either side of Tantra.

"What on earth do the two of you want?" Tantra asked. "It better be fast; I don't need my friends thinking I associate with you."

"We need you to sneak out at midnight tonight and meet us by the oak tree behind Pixie's house," Cinda said. "We have some information you might be interested in. We'll see you there." Cinda and Pixie took off as Tantra stood in the hall, watching them go.

"You were great. Do you think she will actually show up?" asked Pixie.

"I think so. It's kind of suspicious in a bad sort of way, which is right up Tantra's alley," Cinda said. "My mum has left for England so I should be able to sneak out tonight no problem."

"My parents go to bed early so I think I'll be fine too," said Pixie. "What made you change your mind?"

"I guess curiosity got the better of me," Cinda said as the girls walked to the bus. "I am still a little curious about the old woman living in that house. Why would she want to be so far away from everyone?"

"I've been curious about everything too," said Pixie. "I feel like that house and the old woman are linked together. Maybe the old woman knew my grandmother."

"That could be. Maybe that's why your grandmother had that map in the trunk. You being the inquisitive person you are, she probably hoped you would find it. Maybe she wants you to help the old woman," said Cinda.

"This is getting exciting. I'm glad you're into this now; I hope Tantra will be too," said Pixie.

The girls jumped off the bus, agreeing to meet at midnight in the hopes that Tantra would join them.

After Pixie finished supper, she sat down to her harp to practice.

"Pixie, that sounds really good," her father said. "Do you remember that piece you made up that day that made Mr. Bloom run out of here? I would like to hear that one."

"I don't remember any of it, Dad. I'm not sure what I was playing. It was like my fingers took over."

"Please, Parker. Don't bother your daughter with that," said Mrs. Elm. "She's playing so beautiful; it's a perfect way to end the night."

"Alright, alright no more talk of it," said Mr. Elm, looking over at his wife. Pixie finished playing and headed up to her room to do her homework.

It was only 9 p.m. She thought she and Cinda should have planned to meet earlier; a three-hour wait now could put her to sleep. As the time ticked by, Pixie lay in bed with her clothes on and wrote in her journal. I hope Tantra shows up tonight, she thought. Without realizing it, Pixie gradually fell asleep. As she slept, green sparks started hitting her windowsill as they had before on that rainy night. Then a flash of green light lit up her room, waking Pixie in time to get up and meet the girls.

Pixie carefully made her way downstairs without making a sound. She opened the door to the backyard and went outside, headed for the oak tree. She was the first to arrive.

Pixie saw Cinda's back door slowly open as she exited with a flashlight, walking over to Pixie. "Now we just have to wait for Tantra," said Cinda as she sat down.

"Do you think she'll show?" asked Pixie.

"Look, here she comes." Cinda pointed over at Tantra's house, where Tantra was headed out wrapped in a blanket.

"Alright, this better be good, because if you two just got me out of the house at this hour for something stupid, you both are going to get humiliated at school tomorrow," Tantra said as she sat next to Cinda. Pixie and Cinda both looked at each other nervously, hoping what they had to say would be good enough for Tantra.

"I found some things in my grandmother's old trunk that I thought you may be interested in," Pixie said. She handed the article and the old pictures over to Tantra.

"What does this have to do with me?" Tantra asked.

"Tantra, our last names are the same names as some of these people in the article," Cinda said. "Pixie has these old pictures that have our family names listed at the bottom. We seem to have had some kind of connection many years ago."

"Is this some kind of a prank the two of you are trying to pull, because I'm not falling for it," said Tantra as she chucked the article and pictures back at Pixie.

"Do you remember those strange things you found on the trees that you told me about in the woods?" asked Cinda.

"You mean the imprints?" asked Tantra.

"Yes. Pixie's grandmother left a map in her trunk that leads to a house back from the time that article was printed. We followed those marks on the trees. They turned out to be butterfly wings, and they led us through the woods, which helped us find the rest of the trail to the house," said Cinda.

"It's still there," said Pixie.

"That's crazy. What did it look like; was it just a pile of wood?" asked Tantra.

"No, the house was still intact; an old woman lives in it. It's called the House of Charms; the name is still on it just like it is on the map," Pixie said as she handed the map to Tantra.

"Did you talk to the old woman?" asked Tantra.

"No, it was late; we weren't sure if she would be happy to see us or not. But we want to go back and ask her if she knows anything about these things my grandmother kept," Pixie said. "I also found a green dress with a bag of green dust attached to it in the trunk; I'm not sure if it's related in any way."

"Why are you telling me this stuff? Did you talk to your parents?" Tantra asked.

"No, we don't want to do that," Pixie replied. "I think they're trying to hide this from us. My mom would have mentioned it if she wanted me to know."

"We want you to make the trip out with us next time," Cinda said. "Since all three of our families are mentioned in the article, we thought we should include you."

"Gee, thanks. Just what I want to do, head out in the woods to talk to some old woman who will probably think we're nuts."

"Tantra, that mark on the back of your neck, it looks like the shape of a quarter moon," said Cinda, surprised. Pixie looked at it too. She had never seen Tantra close up before.

"Yeah, so what? I've had it forever."

"Me too," said Cinda as she took off her left shoe to show the bottom of her foot. Tantra and Pixie both looked at it. Pixie was in shock as she lifted her arm to show the girls that she also had one in her armpit.

"This is strange. How could we have the same mark?" asked Cinda.

"Well, we must be missing someone," said Tantra.

"What do you mean?" asked Pixie.

"We need another quarter moon to make a full moon," said Tantra. The girls sat in silence, looking at each other and thinking this over.

"I think we really need to take this trip; we should plan it for this weekend," said Pixie.

"That's fine with me," said Cinda.

"Ok, I'm in. But this doesn't mean the two of you are my friends now, so don't come up to me at school and especially don't mention this to anyone," said Tantra as she stood up and walked home.

"That went better than I expected," said Cinda.

"It did. I guess we should head home too," said Pixie.

"Yeah, goodnight. See you tomorrow."

Cinda and Pixie walked back to their houses, unaware of the green, pink and purple sparks lighting up around the oak tree.

Chapter 7

ONE FIREFLY
PER VISIT

Lillian P. Moss

Pixie couldn't wait for the weekend and their adventure, although all three girls acted like they had never met under the oak tree. Pixie wished she could talk to them about it.

She wanted to head out to the House of Charms on Saturday afternoon, but she didn't know how to approach Tantra to let her know. Maybe Cinda would be able to find a way to tell her, thought Pixie. She always had a way of talking to all kinds of different people with no problem, a skill Pixie wished she had.

Friday morning was the start of the school clubs. Pixie couldn't wait to see who signed up for the newspaper this year. She was interested in hearing the topics they would discuss and, of course, if she would be editor in chief again. Her mind kept drifting back to the House of Charms, though.

"Hey, Pixie. We finally get to start the newspaper club. I'm sure you'll be assigned editor in chief again," said Carl as they made their way to the club meeting in Pixie's history classroom.

"I ... yeah, right, that would be nice. I would like that very much," said Pixie, lost in thought about her weekend plans. They entered the classroom and noticed some familiar people: Molly and Jane were already there with twenty other girls surrounding what looked to be Zeb, though Pixie couldn't tell.

"Wow, there is quite a big turnout this year," said Carl. Pixie noticed it was indeed Zeb causing a stir among the group. They were acting like they had never seen a cute guy before. "Great, what's he here for? Can he even make a complete sentence?" Carl asked in a jealous voice.

"He's here to join, just like us," Pixie said. "He is really nice, you know. And, yes, he can form a complete sentence."

"Pixie, I was just telling everyone how I'm looking forward to working on the paper this year and that I thought it would be a great opportunity for me to meet more people, being new and all," Zeb said.

"I think you won't have a problem there, Zeb," said Pixie.

"I'm glad I met you. It's a cool feeling when you meet people you can connect with right away," said Zeb.

"Is that, like, California cool or New York cool?" asked Carl, rolling his eyes.

"Both, I guess," said Zeb, not sure how to respond.

"I'm glad you're joining the club, Zeb," Pixie said. "I think you'll add some spice to the paper this year." While a few girls interrupted Pixie to ask Zeb questions about California and skateboarding, Mrs. Thorn walked in.

Mrs. Thorn was a beautiful black woman who wore her hair tied up in the back and a skirt and blouse combo, a style that she was known for. "Alright, everyone, we have a nice turnout this year. I thought it would be appropriate to start by voting for editor in chief and executive editor," she said. "The editor in chief will be responsible for all decisions, while the executive editor will assist that person. I will pass out cards; please write down the first name you want for editor in chief, and the second name will be your vote for executive editor."

As Mrs. Thorn passed out the cards, Molly leaned over to Pixie. "Isn't it great that Zeb is interested in the paper?" she asked.

"Yes, I'm glad he's here. It should be fun this year," said Pixie.

The group filled out the cards and handed them to Mrs. Thorn, who kept a tally of the votes. After the last one was handed in, Mrs. Thorn stood up and said, "This year it looks like we have a new editor in chief. Congratulations, Mr. Turner."

Zeb looked up in shock. "I wasn't expecting that. Thanks, everyone."

"What? It can't be," said Carl, looking over at Pixie, who seemed a little out of it. Did she hear correctly, her last year in middle school and not getting to be editor in chief again?

"The position of executive editor goes to Pixie Elm," said Mrs. Thorn. Everyone clapped for Zeb and Pixie. "Alright, Zeb, let's get you going on placing assignments. Pixie will help you since she has experience in it."

Pixie went through the motions, carrying herself well even though it did hurt a little. It was obvious that most of the girls had joined the club because they knew Zeb would be there. How could you blame them? Zeb had everything: looks, personality, smarts, and he got along well with everyone. Well, maybe not everyone. Carl seemed to have a dislike for him, which most of the boys outside of Zeb's skater friends did as well. Zeb was a girl magnet and he didn't even know it.

"Pixie, I just want to say that I voted for you to be chief. I'm not sure I'm qualified for the position," Zeb said.

"Zeb, you'll be fine. It's good to change things up. The paper needs a new view. Besides, I'll be there for you."

"Thanks, Pixie. That means a lot." Zeb held Pixie's hand while talking to her, giving her shivers all through her body. She felt just like the other girls in class.

"Let's hand out assignments and put people in groups," said Pixie.

"Sounds good," said Zeb.

"Pixie, can I have a word with you?" asked Mrs. Thorn as the bell rang. Pixie picked up her things and walked over to Mrs. Thorn. "Pixie, are you able to handle this change?"

"I'm fine with it," Pixie said. "Zeb will be a good chief, and I don't mind being second in charge."

"You're a smart girl, Pixie. You show compassion in everything that interests you. Thanks for being a bigger person and not letting this get to you. I'm sure Zeb is going to need a lot of help, so I'm hoping the two of you can pull this together and produce another great year."

"Thanks, Mrs. Thorn. I'm looking forward to it."

"There may be other more important things for you to take care of this year," added Mrs. Thorn as Pixie was leaving.

Pixie thought what Mrs. Thorn said was odd. She walked into the hall where Carl was waiting for her.

"I can't believe what just happened in there. Do you know that Jane and Molly voted for Zeb?" asked Carl.

"It's fine. I'm really okay with it, surprisingly enough. I'll still have some input," Pixie said.

"I can't believe how calm you are about this. Writing is what you love to do."

"Carl, it's OK. I'll see you at lunch," Pixie said. "Oh, wait. Did Joel come up to you at any time wanting to know things about me?"

"You know Joel; he had some English thing he was working on and asked about you. I thought it would be fine since he seemed to be nice about it."

"That's fine; I just wanted to know. Thanks, Carl."

Pixie took off down the hall to her biology class where Zeb was already at their lab table. "You're not upset are you, Pixie?" he asked. "Because that's the last thing I want. We can change titles; it doesn't matter to me."

"Zeb, I want you to be chief. I'm fine with the executive editor position; I'll help you with anything you need. I'm actually looking forward to the change. Change is good, you know," said Pixie.

"Yeah, it is," said Zeb as he squeezed her hand. Pixie felt a tingle shoot up her arm as she smiled back at Zeb.

Pixie's classes seemed to be flying by fast; here she was now sitting in study hall waiting for the bell to go off. The anticipation was killing her. The bell finally rang and she waited until everyone cleared the auditorium to make her move. When the time was right she walked over to the door hidden in the stage.

She quietly opened it, making her way down the stairs to the now familiar hall. This time she noticed something odd: The walls seemed to have grown patches of moss. How could this be, she wondered as she walked quickly to make it to gym class on time. She reached the other side, climbed the steps and opened the door to the closet that now had leaves scattered all over, with a bunch of yard supplies lined up along one wall and a lawn mower in the corner. Pixie thought the whole thing seemed quite odd, but whom could she tell about it? She would probably get in trouble if a teacher found out she was using the secret passage as a quick way to get to her gym class.

Heading out to the hall she bumped into a janitor who had grass stains on his white overalls. He seemed to be singing a strange song about trees coming back to life.

As Pixie walked to her gym class, Tantra, Samantha and Avery, who were waiting for her arrival, greeted her. "Look who finally decided to grace us with her presence," said Avery.

"Poor Pixie, she didn't make chief of the paper this year; it's probably killing her inside," said Samantha.

"I wish I had been there to witness that scene," said Tantra as the three of them laughed at her.

"For your information, I'm fine with it. I have other things that are holding my interest right now, so don't worry about me," said Pixie, looking at Tantra.

"Let's go get ready," Tantra said to Samantha and Avery

The school day seemed like a blur to Pixie as she headed for the bus home. Cinda jumped on the bus and sat next to Pixie. "I just talked to Tantra and told her to meet us at 10:00 in the morning tomorrow; I'm hoping that's fine for you," said Cinda. "I know it's early but I thought that should give us enough time. My mum is coming home tomorrow night, so I must be home early."

"How were you able to get Tantra alone to tell her?" asked Pixie.

"It was easy; I just walked up to her and told her, and she said it was fine."

"I don't know how you do it, but that's great. That time is fine for me too," said Pixie.

The girls said their goodbyes as they left the bus. Cinda needed to get ready for her ballet class, and Pixie, without a harp teacher, decided to spend some time writing in her journal. So many things had happened since finding her grandmother's trunk in the attic. Not making editor in chief really didn't matter to her now. She was more interested in finding out about her past, no matter how long it took. She was doing this for her Grandma Josephine, whom Pixie knew would want her to continue.

The next morning each girl arrived at the oak tree on time. Pixie had her backpack filled with her grandmother's things, bottled water, cups and a flashlight. Cinda brought Phooka along and sandwiches for lunch, just in case they were out late, while Tantra brought a large bag of chips. Pixie packed their things into her backpack and took out the map.

"So, now what?" asked Tantra.

"We follow the trees with the markings and from there we just kind of find it somehow," answered Pixie.

"Let's just get started. I have to be home before 6 tonight; my mum is coming home," said Cinda.

They looked up at the trees once they had arrived at the stream. "There are the markings," said Cinda. "Let's get going." They followed the trees deeper into the woods, coming to a part where the stream crossed their path. Jumping across rocks in the stream, the girls made it to the other side of the forest, getting closer to the House of Charms.

"What's that smell?" asked Tantra.

"I think it's lavender and rosemary," said Cinda. It was so overwhelming that it made the girls completely forget about the map as they followed the scent of the herbs along with the smell of the trees. Feeling alive surrounded by the beautiful forest, the girls ran around collecting herbs, tossing leaves and completely forgetting about the map and why they were there. The forest seemed to get darker as the girls made their way deeper into the woods. The pleasant feeling receded as they reached another part of the stream. The rocks in the stream seemed to illuminate different colors in the water, and they followed them up to the large empty circle of ground that Pixie and Cinda had found earlier. Last time they had felt joy in this spot, but now they felt nothing.

"What happened? I don't feel like myself anymore; I feel a little depressed," said Tantra.

"I'm not sure what it is but the last time Cinda and I were here we felt good, but now not so much," Pixie said.

"Where are we on the map?" asked Cinda.

"I'm not sure; we kind of lost our way while we were playing, but we must be close. This is where we were last time."

"That's just great. Lost in the woods with the two of you. Why did I even agree to this?"

"Oh, Tantra, stop. I'm tired of you always putting us down like you're better than we are," said Cinda.

"Well, I can't help it if I am."

"Please stop. You're being ridiculous right now," said Pixie.

"I think you're the one who's Wait, I think Phooka knows where to go; he's at the other side of the circle waiting for us," said Cinda. The girls stopped arguing and caught up to Phooka.

"I smell a fire up ahead; it must be coming from the House of Charms," said Pixie.

The brush started to get thicker on the other side of the circle as they slowly made their way through the woods. A half-mile later, Phooka led the way as the girls finally made it to the house, which at one time may have been very cute but now looked like an old rundown shack.

"What are we waiting for? Let's go," said Tantra.

"We can't go up there like we were in the neighborhood and just decided to drop by," said Cinda.

"Well, we have to do something now that we're here," said Pixie.

"I've got an idea," said Tantra as she left the two of them and walked up to the old steps, looking up at the House of Charms. Turning around she noticed the others hadn't followed. Tantra shook her head as she approached the door by herself. She knocked and the door mysteriously opened by itself. Tantra jumped back a little, startled. "Are you two coming?" she asked. Pixie and Cinda decided to join her on the porch.

"Should we go in?" asked Cinda.

"I think we should; that's why we're here, to meet the old woman," said Pixie. The girls slowly entered the house, looking around at what seemed to be a shop selling odd things.

"What is this stuff? It's so weird," said Tantra.

There were jars of honey for sale, big cages of butterflies stacked together, baskets of different kinds of gems on the front counter, lilac and rosemary bushes on one side of the wall with bags of river rocks on the other. Tons of herbs, peppermint, licorice roots, berries, mushrooms, walnuts, tree bark, moss, and rainwater in jars were strewn about. Lightning bugs flew around near a sign on the wall saying: "One firefly per visit." They also noticed piles of charcoal on the floor.

"All of this seems familiar to me somehow, but I'm not sure why," said Pixie as she walked around.

"Hello, is anyone here? We've walked a long way and need some assistance," called out Cinda. No one answered.

Tantra set out trying to catch lightning bugs, while Cinda checked out the gems. Pixie spotted a small hallway leading to a room off to the side of the house. "Hey, there's a room down the hallway, maybe someone is in there." she said. The girls slowly walked down the hall, leaving Phooka in the shop, where he was happily smelling everything.

The room was lit by a very large candle in the middle of the floor that cast shadows on the wall.

"Wow, look at all of the pictures. There are tons of them," said Cinda. The drawings were of beautiful women dressed in flowing gowns, with butterflies flitting around wildflowers and trees.

"Is it just me or does it look like these pictures are illuminating some kind of blue sparkly stuff?" asked Pixie.

"They are illuminating blue," said Cinda.

"This place is weird; whoever lives here has to be loony toons," said Tantra.

Then the girls heard the front door open. "Oh, great, now we're stuck here with some lunatic," whispered Tantra, scaring Cinda. The girls listened as they heard a boy's voice talking to Phooka.

"Hey, there, boy. How did you get in here?" Phooka looked up at the boy, licking his leg and giving a small bark of joy. "Don't worry, this sort of thing happens all the time. That's all we get around here -- lost animals."

Cinda tried to get a look at the boy while walking slowly across the room toward the doorway. "Cinda, watch out," Pixie whispered as Cinda tripped on some charcoal and fell to the floor. The three girls stood in silence, not knowing what to do. The boy was silent as well.

Walking slowly down the hall and holding a broomstick appeared a tall, slim, attractive boy with long, black hair and a tan complexion. "Hello, can I help you with something?" he asked.

Pixie decided to step out and show they meant no harm. "Hello, I'm sorry we entered your home uninvited, but the door seemed to open by itself," said Pixie. The boy stared at the girls, acting like he had never seen other people up close before.

"My name is Pixie. This is Cinda." Cinda said hello and started blushing. "And that is Tantra."

"Hi, my name is Noon," the boy said. "Sorry if I seem awkward; we just never get visitors as far as I know."

The girls noticed how Noon was dressed and guessed he was probably right. He seemed to be wearing some kind of burlap material. Even though his clothes were odd, the girls couldn't help but look at him; he was definitely cute.

"Do you live here by yourself, Noon, or do you share the house with someone else?" asked Pixie.

"I live here with my mother. She's probably upstairs right now in the library. She can't hear or see that well anymore."

"Why don't you go to school like us?" asked Tantra.

"My mom doesn't want me to wander too far from the house or talk to strangers. She's afraid something may happen to me, or her. So I stay close to protect her."

"Noon, what's your mom's name?" asked Pixie.

"Her name is Lillian P. Moss," said Noon. "What's the dog's name?"

"His name is Phooka," said Cinda shyly.

"That's a great name," Noon said as he played with Phooka. "I think I've seen it somewhere."

Pixie took off her backpack and showed Noon her grandmother's newspaper clippings, pictures and the map she had found in the trunk. "I have these things of my grandmother's; she passed away and left them in a trunk, and that is why we are here. Those people in that picture have the same last names as we do. The map led us here." Noon was listening, but he was also looking at the article in disbelief. There, pictured alone back in the 1800s, was a woman who looked exactly like his mother. Under the picture was a name: Lillian P. Moss.

"I'm not sure what any of this means; I'm not even sure my mom would know, either." Noon gave the papers back to Pixie, who looked a little disappointed.

"What is this place? Is this a store; and why are you selling all these weird things?" asked Tantra.

"She's the friendly one," Pixie said as Tantra gave her a look.

"It is a store; we supply all these things for people who need them," said Noon.

"Like who?" asked Tantra.

"I'm not sure, I've never seen anyone come in, but I'm always going out looking to refill our stock," Noon said.

"That's just weird," Tantra said.

A voice from above shouted down, "Noon, are you talking to someone down there? Who's there?"

"We have visitors. Three girls, and they have some pictures and things that they want to ask you about," Noon said.

Then Lillian P. Moss walked down the stairs. A beautiful old black woman with white streaks running through her hair, Lillian wore a long red dress and a purple robe. She had a pair of old circle-rimmed glasses and a necklace that seemed to be missing stones. She looked at the girls and smiled.

"Nopoon gopo gopet thope op bopook," said Lillian to Noon in a language unfamiliar to the girls. Noon took off up the stairs while Lillian entered the room to get a closer look at the girls.

"Let me see these things that you have," Lillian said.

Pixie handed over the pictures and the map. The girls watched as Lillian smiled. "These things are your grandmother's?" she asked.

"Yes," said Pixie. "I found them in a trunk of hers after she passed away."

"Well, I guess I do have many stories to share and secrets that need to be told, if you're interested," Lillian said to the girls.

"Listen, lady, what is this place?" asked Tantra with her hands on her hips. "Why do we have a map and pictures with our last names? What is the connection between us and this place?"

Lillian smiled. "In due time you will know it all; things like this cannot be rushed. Does anyone else know about this, or that the three of you are here?" asked Lillian.

"No, we've kept it to ourselves; we don't think it's something our parents want us to know about," said Cinda.

"Very good, very good; let's keep it that way for now."

Noon came downstairs carrying a brown book that looked like it was made of bark. The cover had the word "OPISH" printed on it in gold shimmery letters. The pages looked burnt around the edges. "Here, take this book, read through it and come back when you understand it," said Lillian.

Lillian handed the book to Pixie as she walked away from them and back up the stairs. She muttered as she left: "You'll see as it all happens."

Noon and the girls watched as Lillian disappeared back into the library. "I hope you take the time to look through that book; it may answer some of your questions," said Noon. "Please come back sometime. My mom will explain more to you then. She gets tired easily and needs to rest often. I'm sorry she wasn't able to answer anything now."

"Who says we want to come back, anyway," said Tantra.

"Tantra, be quiet for once," said Cinda. "It was nice meeting you, Noon. I would love to see you again." Cinda held out her hand and Noon shook it.

"Likewise," he said as he smiled at her.

"Oh, brother, I see what's going on here. Can we just go now?" Tantra said to Pixie as she grabbed Cinda.

"Yes. Thanks, Noon. I'll take a look at the book and come back to meet for a talk with your mom again," said Pixie.

As Pixie opened her backpack to put the book back inside, Tantra grabbed the big bag of chips from it and handed them to Noon.

"Here, this is something we buy in stores. It's good; you eat it," Tantra said.

Pixie waved bye to Noon as the three left the house with Phooka following. Cinda walked backward, continuing to smile at Noon while being dragged out of the door by Tantra. Noon was smiling back.

Chapter 8

OP Language

Phooka led the way as the girls followed the map out of the woods. "That was crazy weird. I have no desire to go back there anytime soon, just to let you know. And while we're on the subject, don't even mention any of this to my friends. As far as you remember I wasn't even there," Tantra said.

"That's fine," Pixie said to Tantra just to get her to shut up.

"I may want to go back, so let me know when you do," Cinda said to Pixie.

"Of course you do. I'm surprised you didn't ask him out," Tantra said to Cinda in disgust.

"That's not why. I'm interested in finding out what all of this means," Cinda said. "Like maybe you should be too."

"Yeah, right," said Tantra.

"Would the two of you stop it? Let's just get out of here and go home. I want to check this book out," said Pixie.

The girls made it to the stream, where they hopped the rocks back onto the other side of the woods, then crossed the stream again leading to the bridge that took them to the trail home. Pixie couldn't wait to take a look at the book; she wondered if it held the answers to her questions.

Tantra turned to Cinda and Pixie and said, "No more crazy trips, so don't bother me anymore." Then she walked to her house.

"She's so nasty; I really don't know how she lives with herself," said Cinda. "I have to be heading home too; my dad and I are picking up my mum at the airport soon. I can't wait to find out how her trip went, and maybe I will be able to find out why she really went out there. I think it was more than just visiting her friends."

"I'll talk to you later, and I'll let you know what I've found out from the book," Pixie said.

"Sounds great. Oh, Pixie, about Noon -- I do think he's kind of cute. Do you think he might have thought I was too?"

"If the way he smiled at you while we were leaving was any indication of how he felt, I'd say it's pretty good odds that he thought you were 'all that,' " Pixie said.

"Ha, ha, very funny. I do think he may have liked me, though. I guess I'll find out on our next visit. Ta-ta for now."

Cinda and Phooka took off for home, while Pixie headed to the back door of her house. Pixie's parents were in the living room reading the paper when she entered.

"Hey, how was your picnic with the girls?" Pixie's father asked. "I'm glad you're becoming friends with that other girl too; what's her name again?"

"Her name is Tantra, Dad, and, yeah, we had fun. It was a beautiful day for a walk in the woods, we talked about school and boys, you know, stuff like that."

"That sounds like fun. Oh, your grandparents are on their way over for dinner tonight; you know they will want you to play the harp. Just a fair warning," said Mrs. Elm.

"That's fine. I'm going upstairs to start my homework. I have a lot this weekend."

"That's my girl, always on top of her studies," said Mr. Elm.

Pixie headed up to her room and closed her door, then opened her backpack to look at the book.

She had never heard of Opish. Could it be the language that Lillian was speaking to Noon at the House of Charms? She wondered if it was used in the 1800s by the people in the photos; maybe it was code. She examined the book's cover, which was crafted out of bark. The word "Opish" looked like it was etched with a file and then filled with some kind of glitter. The gold let off a vibrant glow.

Pixie slowly opened the book, a little fearful of what she might find. The first page, like the rest, looked like it was made from onionskin; it had a tan, tea-stained look, with the edges of the pages burnt. She had never seen anything like it before.

The title page seemed to be written in the Op language: "Thope Lopangopuagope oopf thope sopecropet sopocopiety." Pixie stared at this for a while. "Great," she thought, "What does this mean?" She flipped through the pages and noticed that the whole book was written like that. How would she ever figure this out? It was impossible to read.

Frustrated, she closed the book and lay down on her bed. "Please let me figure this out. I need to get this, or this whole adventure was for nothing," she thought. "I can't go back to Lillian P. Moss without knowing what the book was about. She will be very disappointed and probably won't give out any more information."

She wished Noon were here with her now to explain it to her. He was nice enough at the house, she thought. He would definitely help her. Pixie sat up in bed and picked up the book again. "I'll just look at it till I solve it," she thought. "Maybe it's like solving a puzzle." Pixie began to read the title over and over again until she could speak it fluently. She started out slowly, trying to pronounce the words just right. By the fifteenth time of repeating the title something magical happened. All the "ops" from it floated up in the air like golden sparkles all around her. She was surrounded by ops.

Pixie, spooked by what happened and in total disbelief, looked down at the title again and there, written in English, was: "The Language of the Secret Society."

It was crazy. She had heard of magic, of course, but never thought anything like this could happen. She wondered why the people who wrote the book had to be so secretive.

Pixie flipped through the pages, realizing it might take awhile for her to decode the language. It was definitely a puzzle that she was excited to have cracked.

"Pixie, Grandma and Grandpa are here. Why don't you come downstairs and play something on the harp," Mrs. Elm called up the stairs.

"I'll be right down, Mom."

Oh no, thought Pixie, how am I supposed to get rid of the floating ops? The ops were scattered all around her room. They were on her bookshelves, on top of her computer, floating in her closet. She would never know how to explain this to her parents.

"Pixie, are you coming?" called her mom.

"Yes, Mom, I'll be right there." Pixie could hear her mom climbing the stairs, and she decided to close the book fast and hide it under a loose floorboard in her closet. To her surprise all of the ops followed the book once it was closed. She put the book in the hole and covered it with the floorboard just in time.

"Pixie, you know, I think you should play that piece Mr. Bloom taught you on your last lesson; it was so pretty."

Pixie opened her door. "I've got it right here."

"Great," said Pixie's mom. "I'm almost done with dinner. It will be nice to have some entertainment before we eat."

Pixie ran down the stairs with her sheet music and kissed her grandparents.

"Hey, there, sweetheart. How is school going for you this year?" asked her grandfather. Did you make editor in chief again?"

"School is going good. I like all my teachers and the classes are interesting, but I didn't make editor in chief this year."

"What? You didn't tell us," said Mrs. Elm. "What happened? Why did you keep that from us?"

Mr. Elm looked shocked.

"I must have forgotten; but it's really no big deal. I made executive editor. I'm second in command."

"But, Pixie, you've been doing that paper for three years now and you've always been editor in chief. This is something you want to do after college. Who do I need to talk to?" asked Mr. Elm.

"No one, dad. I need a break from it this year anyway. I want to concentrate on my schoolwork."

"That's my girl; put school first," said Pixie's grandpa.

"Pixie, play us a song," said Pixie's grandma, smiling. You know how Grandpa and I just love to hear you play."

Pixie sat at the harp and began to play. She started to get that weird feeling again like her fingers were moving without her; she felt disconnected from her hands. And then, there it was again, the feeling of separation from her body. What was she playing? It was that trees song again. Pixie's mom seemed to turn white. While watching Pixie play she noticed green sparks glowing off the strings. Looking around, Mrs. Elm was relieved that no one else seemed to notice.

"Dinner is ready now. I think we should all take our seats. Come everyone; I made a special meal and I don't want it to get cold." Mrs. Elm jumped up and ran to the kitchen to get everything ready.

"Do you need help, Jill?" asked Pixie's grandma as she got up and walked toward the kitchen.

"I'm going to go wash my hands; I'll be right down," said Pixie as she sprinted up the stairs.

"I guess the show is over, Pop," said Pixie's dad. "You want to help set the table with me?"

"Sure," said Pixie's grandpa as he headed into the kitchen with his son.

Pixie ran up to her room to collect the newspaper article, pictures and map to return them to her grandmother's trunk. She felt she needed to put them back before her mom was onto her and found them missing. Opening the attic door slowly, she walked across the room and unlocked the old trunk. As she lifted the lid, she took a look inside at the green dress and the odd dust in the mesh bag. Pixie wondered about the dress. Was it her grandmother's? And what about that strange bag? Placing the papers back in the trunk, she closed it back up and locked it.

Back in her room, Pixie decided to put the key under the floorboard with the Opish book.

"Pixie, dinner is being served. Come on down," yelled her dad.

Sitting at the dinner table with her family, all Pixie could think about was the book hidden in her room. She wanted to spend the night going through it to figure out what it was about.

At dinner, her parents and grandparents talked about the house, trips they wanted to take and her dad's job. Pixie decided to sneak away early, asking to be excused from the dinner table. She kissed her grandparents and then headed up to her room.

Shutting her bedroom door behind her, she sprinted to the closet and lifted the loose floorboard to retrieve the book. She relaxed on her bed and opened it to a page that seemed to be the table of contents. Now that she knew how the book worked the chapters appeared: how to build butterfly houses; cooking with herbs and other things found in a forest; transformational properties of gems and minerals; how to find a perfect location; trees and their importance; humus-rich soil; arranging the perfect environment; how to blend into the background; and keeping your secrets.

Pixie began to read the first chapter about building butterfly houses. As she deciphered the language, all the ops began to fly off the pages and float around her room once again. She was too busy reading to even notice them.

Pixie couldn't believe it: Everything in the chapter on how to build butterfly houses was basically what she was doing already in her woodworking class. How could I know all of this, she thought. As Pixie finished the chapter she closed the book and the ops formed a line as they magically disappeared back inside.

She moved on to the next chapter about cooking with herbs. Recipes were given along with a list of herbs and other ingredients and where to find them. Pixie recognized many things that the House of Charms sold in the shop. If they're selling these things in the shop, she thought, there must be families still living this communal life, as Noon mentioned he is always going out to replenish supplies.

Pixie continued taking notes on each chapter until she noticed the time and figured she could get in one more chapter before bed. Pixie headed to her door to hear if her family was still downstairs talking. They were so she sat back on her bed and started the next chapter on the transformational properties of gems and minerals.

The first stone that caught her eye was the emerald: "Strengthens heart, liver, immune system, and tonic for body/mind/spirit. Enhances dreams, deep spiritual insight, emotional balance, tranquility, love and prosperity." Pixie felt this stone represented her; she had always loved the color green.

She also came across the rose quartz and thought this stone represented Cinda: "aids circulatory system, increases fertility, helps stored anger and resentment, reduces stress, self-confidence, creativity, forgiveness, compassion and love."

Pixie was having fun matching the gems to the appropriate person each represented. Lapis lazuli, turquoise, amethyst -- Pixie noticed that whenever Tantra had her high-tops on she always wore purple shoelaces, and her skateboard had purple wheels. The amethyst was Tantra's stone: "strengthens immunity, purifies/ energizes, transformation, psychic abilities, inspiration and intuition."

She looked through the list to find a gem for Noon. Remembering that his room was illuminated blue from the chalk he used for his drawings she picked the sapphire: "aligns body/mind/spirit, enhances psychic abilities, loyalty, truth and love."

Now on to the woman herself. Pixie checked the stones and found the perfect one for Lillian P. Moss; it was the ruby: "strengthens the physical/spiritual heart, banishes limitations, courage, selfless service, joy, devotion, power, and leadership." Without knowing much about Lillian, the ruby seemed to be the perfect match for her spirit.

A knock on her door startled Pixie back to the real world as she closed the book and ran to the closet to put it back under the floorboard.

"Pixie, we're all going to bed now; come out and say goodnight to your grandparents," her mother said.

Pixie opened the door and hugged her mom as she made her way to the guest room to kiss her grandparents. "See you in the morning; sleep tight," her grandmother said.

"I will, Grandma."

Changing into her pajamas and brushing her teeth Pixie thought about the book, wanting to call Cinda and tell her about her findings. She only had six more chapters left that she hoped to finish in two days. The faster she finished the book, the sooner she could make her next trip to the House of Charms. Lying down in bed, her thoughts were on the house, Lillian, and Noon.

Drifting slowly to sleep, Pixie started to dream about a family living in the woods, gathering around a fire at night, singing songs and playing drums as the children danced. Everyone was happy. The fire pit was glowing and one of the women scooped out soup and placed it in wooden bowls that were passed around. Everyone was dressed in beautiful, radiant colors. The young girls all wore dresses that sparkled, while the boys wore pants to the knees and a top that seemed to be made of burlap material that also sparkled. The parents laughed and clapped as they watched the children dance. It was a pleasant dream, sending Pixie into a deep sleep.

Meanwhile, Mrs. Elm tossed and turned thinking about Pixie and that song she kept playing on the harp. Tonight while Pixie played, Mrs. Elm had noticed the green sparks. Why was it happening; why now? All of those things had been buried when her mother passed away. The trunk. It had to be her mother's wooden trunk in the attic causing this. She wished she could get rid of it, but it did hold a lot of childhood memories. She remembered playing in the dress while her mom sang the trees song to her. It was also in her mother's will that she had to keep the trunk and eventually pass it down to Pixie.

Did Pixie find the trunk and open it? How could she? The key was lost years ago. The only other way to open it was by repeating her mother's name three times in Opish. How would Pixie know how to do that? Mrs. Elm had to check out the trunk for herself.

Slowly getting out of bed and trying not to wake her husband, she slipped out of the room and up to the attic. Making her way to the far corner, she uncovered the trunk. She placed her hands on top of it and repeated her mother's name three times in Opish: "Joposopephopinope Opelm." The trunk clicked open, and Mrs. Elm lifted the lid to make sure everything was still there: books that her mom would read to her when she was young with make believe stories, the pictures of ancestors, the newspaper clippings, the old map and her childhood play dress were all still there.

The dust seemed to have lost its sparkle; it looked like it was dying. Why could that be? She thought of

Dana, Cinda's mother, taking her trip to England to find her dress. Tantra's parents probably got rid of their dress because of the terrible thing that happened during Tantra's birth.

Mrs. Elm picked up the map. It had been 12 years since she, Dana, and the Birches had made the trip to the House of Charms. Could the house still be there after all this time?

Mrs. Elm decided to put everything back in the trunk, closing it the same way she opened it. She made her way back to her room without a sound. Feeling like she had control of the situation, Mrs. Elm soon fell sound asleep.

In the next room, Pixie woke up suddenly, sneaking out of bed to get her journal and flashlight to write about the vivid dream she had just had. Just as she was closing her eyes to sleep again, she saw something on the window out of the corner of her eye. Pixie turned to face the window just in time to notice green sparks hitting it. She got out of bed groggily to look out the window, but nothing was there. Maybe she was just imagining it, she thought.

Not thinking much more about it, Pixie got back to bed and fell back into her dream, back around the fire watching everyone enjoying the evening. Oh, how nice, she thought, as she drifted deeper into sleep.

Chapter 9

Flying Girl, Pink Hair and Bad Dreams

The next morning Pixie woke up in good spirits. She wanted to hurry and meet with Cinda to tell her about the Opish book and about the dream that had felt so real. She wished she could share everything with her mom and dad, but she felt the time wasn't right yet. She was sure that once Cinda read through the book, she definitely would want to go back to the House of Charms with her, if not to meet with Lillian then definitely to see Noon again. Pixie wasn't so sure she could get Tantra to join them since she had told them to leave her out of it.

Pixie got out of bed and started getting ready to head downstairs and have breakfast with her family, who were all sitting around the kitchen table with stacks of warm pancakes, maple syrup, and powdered sugar laid out, accompanied by hot tea.

"You're up and dressed early this morning; what gives us the honor of your presence?" Mr. Elm asked.

"Oh, Dad, I'm always up early. I just wanted to get dressed so I could go over and visit with Cinda this morning before she takes off for ballet class. Her mom just got back from England, so I wanted to ask about the trip."

Pixie's mom looked up as she passed the pancakes around the table. "After breakfast I would like to take a walk over, too. I want to see how Dana made out on her trip," said Mrs. Elm. "Pixie, I'll join you."

"That would be fine, Mom," Pixie said, hoping she would get a chance to talk to Cinda in private.

After breakfast, Pixie followed her mom out the door. "Hey, Mom, do you have any relatives who live around here?" she asked.

"Pixie, you know that I don't. I'm an only child and your grandmother was an only child and so was her mother and father. My father, your grandfather, had a brother we lost contact with many years ago. Why do you ask?"

"I was just wondering if I had any family around that I didn't know about."

"You know everyone from your father's side; that's our family," said Mrs. Elm.

The Willow's front door opened as they approached the house, and Mr. Willow greeted Mrs. Elm and Pixie.

"Good morning, fine ladies. I guess you're here to inquire about the Willow women; you will find them in the kitchen having a spot of tea."

"Good morning, neighbors. Don't mind him; he's just having fun with me," Mrs. Willow said. "He says my accent gets stronger every time I come back from a visit from England. Come on in both of you."

"So, Dana, how was your trip?" said Mrs. Elm.

"Oh, just fine. It was nice seeing everyone. I love visiting; it's such a nice comfort to go back home for a visit."

Pixie followed Phooka up the stairs to Cinda's room, where she was sitting at her vanity table putting her hair in a bun for ballet class.

"Good morning, Pixie," said Cinda in a solemn voice.

"What's the matter with you?" asked Pixie.

"Something has happened to my hair. I'm trying to hide it in the bun but I'm not sure what to do about it. It put a fright in my mum when she saw it this morning. I think it has to do with us going to that House of Charms place," said Cinda.

"What's the matter with it?" asked Pixie.

Cinda shook her hair out to reveal thin pieces of pink strands mixed in with the blond.

"Did you color it like that?" asked Pixie.

"Of course I didn't. I've tried washing it three times now; it doesn't come out," said Cinda.

"Well, it's not noticeable; it looks like it's only a few pieces," said Pixie.

"That's not the point. Why do I have it? Where did it come from?"

"Why do you think it happened because of our visit to the House of Charms? Nothing happened to me," said Pixie.

"I haven't done anything odd except that, so what do you figure?" asked Cinda.

"Are you mad at me? Did you tell your mom about the House of Charms?"

"I'm not sure about the first question, and no, of course not, to the second."

"Cinda, I'm sorry. I didn't do anything to cause your hair to turn pink. I just don't believe visiting a place could have that effect on someone."

"Well, I can't explain it. Thank goodness it's not that noticeable; I'm not sure what I would do if it were."

"Did your mom say anything when she saw it?" asked Pixie.

"No, she just helped me try to wash it out."

Cinda put her hair back in a bun, sticking the pink strands inside.

"I know it's weird, but at least it's your favorite color," Pixie said. Cinda looked at Pixie and rolled her eyes. "Sorry," said Pixie.

"I can't find any humor in this right now," said Cinda.

"How was your mom's visit to England?" Pixie asked, changing the subject. "She seems to be in good spirits."

"She is … except I caught her talking to my dad and she seemed very upset about something. I'm not sure what they were talking about, but I think it has to do with something she was unable to find there. My dad consoled her and told her it was all right; if it wanted to be found, she would have found it. He said something about the timing not being right."

"That's weird; I wonder what she could have been looking for." Pixie said.

"Other than that she had a great time with her friends."

"Well, that's good," Pixie said. "I'm not sure you care right now, but I've started to read that book Lillian gave me. It's called 'Opish' and it's in some strange language that I think we heard Lillian speaking to Noon. It took me awhile to figure it out, but the oddest thing happened when I did: All of these 'ops' started floating off the pages as I read. There were so many floating in my room, and if I shut the book they disappeared back into the pages. I want you to come over to see it one night."

"What are ops?" asked Cinda.

"It seems to be a language that puts the letters 'o' and 'p' in front of vowels to make a code."

"What was the book about?"

"So far I've learned how to make butterfly houses, how to cook with herbs, and information about gems. I think it's some kind of a commune-type living guide," said Pixie.

"That might explain the pictures of those families; maybe they all lived together in the woods away from other people," said Cinda. "So you don't believe that the House of Charms turned my hair pink, even after witnessing flying letters in your room?"

"I guess it is out of the ordinary," said Pixie.

"I'm not sure I want to go back to that place again; it's freaky. I'm scared we may be involved in something we shouldn't be," said Cinda.

"I don't think my grandmother was involved in anything weird," Pixie said. "I don't think the House of Charms is bad or Lillian, either, for that matter. It's a part of our past that I'm interested in, and we have access to it right in our backyard."

"That's fine; you go and let me know your findings. I don't want to go back."

"OK, as long as we can still talk about it; I can't share this with anyone else. I guess when I go back after I finish the book I'll tell Noon you said hi but won't be stopping by again because you think where he lives is freaky."

"Don't you dare say that," Cinda said. "If you can solve my pink hair problem I'll go back to visit the House of Charms with you. If not, I'm out."

"Cinda," called Mrs. Willow. "We should get going for your class; do you have everything you need?"

"Yes, Mum, I'll be down in a minute."

"I'll keep you informed of my findings, and if I come across a cure for pink hair I'll pass it your way," Pixie said.

"Yeah, thanks," said Cinda, rolling her eyes.

The girls headed downstairs. Pixie's mom had already left. Pixie said her goodbyes as she headed back home in hopes of going through more chapters. As she was just about to open the kitchen door she overheard her mom talking to her dad about Mrs. Willow's trip to England. Curiosity got the better of her and she decided to listen, crouching down so as not to be seen.

"Parker, you don't understand how important it is that she finds it. Without it, who knows what may happen," said Mrs. Elm.

"Why was it gone in the first place if it was so important?" asked Mr. Elm.

"Our parents were young then; her mother didn't want to be associated with it because of fear."

"Well, why is it important now?" asked Mr. Elm.

"I think it's dying. I saw it last night; it doesn't look good. I told Dana about it and she's upset."

"What about the other one; is that still around?"

"I'm pretty sure it is. I'm positive it's dying as well."

"There is nothing that can change who you are as long as you keep it in your heart," said Mr. Elm.

Just as Mr. Elm said this Pixie opened the door. "What's going on? Is everything all right? I thought I heard you two talking about something dying," asked Pixie.

Mrs. Elm turned white as she looked at Pixie. "Oh, it's nothing, honey. Just some plants that Dana and I want to try to grow that seem to be having a hard time of it."

"OK, I hope you have better luck then," said Pixie as she left the kitchen and headed for the living room to spend time with her grandparents before they left.

"Do you think she knows, Parker?" asked Mrs. Elm when Pixie had gone.

"No, I don't think she knows, but I think you should sit down and talk to her about it. I think it would be in your best interest to tell her."

"I can't; we made a pact not to tell the kids. Not right now anyway."

"You must do it sometime soon if you're worried about what may happen."

"I know, I know. I'll talk to Dana about it," Mrs. Elm said.

Just then they could hear Pixie's grandma in the other room: "Pixie, play your harp for us one last time before we take off, will you, honey?"

"Sure." Pixie got up and decided to play without her sheet music to see what would happen. As she started, she felt it again -- the feeling that something was taking over as she started to play that trees song. She didn't even know if it was about trees; it just felt like it was. Her mom and dad entered the room and Pixie looked up at her parents. Her mom looked nervous, making Pixie lose the strange song.

"Oh, that's such a pretty melody, Pixie. One day you'll have to play it all the way through," her grandma said.

"I would like to, Grandma, but I don't know how it goes. I was just playing around."

"Well, it's beautiful just the same," said her grandpa as he got up. "We should be on our way if we want to get back at a reasonable time, Son."

99

"Sure, Dad, that's fine. We have to do this more often; we enjoy having the both of you here with us," said Mr. Elm.

"Likewise," said Grandma.

The family helped gather the luggage and other belongings and loaded up the car. They said their goodbyes as Pixie and her parents watched the two of them take off in their old pale blue Beetle down Cedar Wood Way.

"I guess I'll start my homework now," said Pixie as she turned back to the front door.

"Where did you learn that song, Pixie?" asked Mr. Elm.

"I don't know; sometimes when I sit at the harp something comes over me and I lose myself in the music and my fingers just do what they want. It's really weird."

"OK, Pixie. Go up and finish your homework before we have dinner," said Mrs. Elm.

Happy to escape to her room, Pixie closed the door and locked it before she opened the floorboard to get the Opish book out. She headed to her bed to read through more of the chapters.

Pixie opened to Chapter Four on "Poperfopect Lopocopatopion." After saying it a few times, she was able to make the ops fly off the page, leaving the words "Perfect Location." The chapter explained how to find a location in the woods that would supply all your living needs. The quality of life around the circle had to be perfect for a peaceful life. You were not to change the environment to fit your needs, but to find an environment that was already suitable for you.

The next two chapters talked about the importance of trees, growth of trees, age of trees and different types of trees in the area that are good for happiness. Also, the importance of bees and other such insects for pollination and humus-rich soil. The soil had to be perfect to create the perfect living ring. Make sure there are plenty of mushrooms around the area, added the author.

Pixie's bedroom was completely filled with small floating ops as she finished Chapter Six. She laid her head on her pillow for a moment to think about what she had just read. She slowly fell into a deep sleep and the recurring dream came back to her: It was another beautiful night in the woods and she was sitting on a hammock with two other girls. The three of them were watching the festivities around the fire. A few people were playing drums, wooden flutes and tambourines while others danced. Mostly it was the small children dancing around the fire, while the others helped in cooking a meal of fruits and vegetables. The huts surrounding the circle looked like large mushrooms. The feeling was joyous and loving until her dream took a turn for the worse.

Fires were suddenly all around. Huts were burning and people were screaming as they tried to find a way to escape. The sounds of gunfire could be heard, and the joyful people in her pleasant dream were being killed. Pixie was frightened for her life in the dream; her two best friends were with her hiding inside an old hollowed-out log. They watched as the people they loved fell all around. Pixie and the two girls clung to one another as they cried.

Pixie woke with a jolt, covered in sweat from the nightmare. The dream had felt so real. She wiped a tear from her eye, the same tear that she had shed in the dream. Then she became startled by knocks on her door.

"Pixie, are you alright? I thought I heard you crying," asked Mrs. Elm. "Dinner is almost ready. Open the door, Pixie." Pixie quickly closed the book and put it under the floorboard where the ops followed. She then opened the door to face her mom.

"Sorry, Mom. I had such a bad dream. I must have fallen asleep while studying. It was so sad; people were dying and there was so much hate."

"Oh, Pixie, it's fine now; it was only a dream," said Mrs. Elm as she hugged her daughter.

"It felt so real."

"Dreams sometimes do. Come downstairs. I made your favorite: stuffed peppers."

Pixie headed downstairs with her mom to the kitchen where her father was already at the table. "What happened; is everything alright? I thought I heard screaming and crying," said Mr. Elm.

"Everything is fine, Parker. Just a bad dream, that's all."

"Pixie, you put a fright in me. I thought something bad happened," her dad said.

"It did, Dad. Nice people were being killed in my dream, I think just because they were different."

"That's terrible. With all the pleasant things going on in your life, how could something like this pop up?"

"I'm not sure, Dad; it just did. I felt like I was there."

"Pixie, it didn't happen for real so please let's talk of something pleasant to get your mind away from it," said Mrs. Elm.

"Yeah, good idea," Mr. Elm said. "So how did the homework go? Did you finish it all?" Pixie realized she hadn't done any homework all weekend. She had never forgotten to do her homework before.

"Almost, Dad. I think I should go up and finish right after dinner."

"Good idea. We want to keep on top of things," said Mr. Elm.

Pixie had so much homework to do that night that she had to pick the most important things to work on first. She started biology first because she didn't want to let Zeb down by not doing her part as his lab partner. After that, she had time to do some math problems and write in her journal for English class. Everything else she would have to find time to catch up on during school the next day.

That night Pixie's dreams took her back to the fires, where people were screaming and she could hear and feel everything that was happening from her hiding spot with the two other girls. They decided to make a run for it, heading deeper into the woods when it seemed to be silent outside the hollow log. As they took off running a large storm began, sending a downpour of rain and lightning that filled the night sky. The girls held hands as they ran through the woods, wet from the rain, getting farther and farther from the terrible scene. They helped each other across a small stream by hopping on the large rocks that led them to the other side. Bushes scraped their arms as they made their way to a trail they knew well.

The rain kept pouring down as they looked ahead at a small house with lit candles inside and the smell of firewood burning. It was hard to see clearly but Pixie knew where they were going.

The girls took off running to the house, and Pixie woke up, sweating and shaking. She got out of bed and noticed that her hair and pajamas were completely drenched. She pulled up her sleeves and saw small scrapes across her arms. How could this be? It was just a dream; why was she wet? She went to her bathroom to towel off her hair and change into fresh pajamas. She couldn't tell her parents; they wouldn't believe her. Maybe Cinda was right: The House of Charms could have caused her pink hair, and now Pixie was experiencing bad, life-like dreams. She wondered if anything was happening to Tantra. All she could think of was how this was all her fault. She should have left the trunk alone or asked her mom about it when she first found it.

It was too late now. She had to finish the Opish book and go back to the House of Charms to find out what was happening. Pixie fought off sleep as best as she could by tossing and turning the rest of the night.

The next morning Pixie woke up exhausted. She took a shower, hoping it would help make her feel awake, but it didn't change anything.

"Look at you; you look exhausted. Did you get any sleep last night?" asked Pixie's mom when Pixie came downstairs.

"Not much, I guess. I have a lot going on with school this year."

"That's not good. I want you to go right to bed tonight as soon as you finish your homework. Pixie, you can't go to school like this every day."

"I won't, Mom. It was just last night; I had another bad dream, that's all. I should head out now or I may miss the bus."

"Take a cereal bar with you and water; you need to eat something."

"Alright, Mom."

Pixie headed outside and noticed that Cinda was already waiting. She was wearing a beret with her hair up. Pixie could guess what was under that hat before Cinda said anything.

"Hey, Cinda," Pixie said. Cinda just looked at her.

"What's wrong with you?" asked Cinda.

"Nothing, I just couldn't get to sleep last night so I'm really tired."

"Well, guess what has happened to me this morning?" asked Cinda.

"Don't tell me, your hair is now completely pink?"

"I know you find humor in this but I don't know what to do about it. The pink streaks are thicker. I can't get it out at all. I'm not the kind of girl who would dye my hair pink just for the fun of it. How do I explain it?"

"Just say it's for your dance class and they wanted you to have pink hair for a performance."

"That's not going to work. I'll probably get kicked out of dance because of it."

"I'm planning on going to meet with Lillian soon to find out what to do. I'm sorry; I didn't think anything like this would happen to us," said Pixie.

"What do you mean 'us'? What has happened to you?" asked Cinda.

"I've been having really bad dreams where I'm actually there. I woke up last night completely wet because in my dream I was running through the woods in a rain storm."

"That is freaky. I guess you now believe this has to do with that house," Cinda said.

"Yeah, I think you're right. I'm worried to see what has happened to Tantra. I'm surprised we didn't get any angry calls from her yet," said Pixie.

The bus was making its way to their stop right as Tantra skated down her front ramp to make it just in time. Pixie and Cinda watched as she got closer, but nothing seemed out of sorts with her.

During the ride to school, Pixie fell sound sleep only to be woken up what seemed like a few minutes later as Cinda shook her. "I can't believe we're here already. I'm so tired; all I want to do is go back to bed," said Pixie.

Tantra pushed her way through the aisle with a couple of her friends and skated off the bus to school. Pixie noticed there was something odd about Tantra but she wasn't sure if she was just hallucinating from lack of sleep.

"Cinda, is it just me or is Tantra flying above her skateboard?"

"Oh, my, she is flying about a good inch above her skateboard! I can't believe no one has noticed it," said Cinda.

"I can't believe *she* hasn't noticed," said Pixie.

"Well, let's not be the ones to tell her. Agreed?"

"Agreed," said Pixie.

Pixie struggled to stay awake in her classes. She found out about a test in history class that she had forgotten to study for, making her feel sick. There was nothing she could do but hand it in knowing she did poorly.

One good thing about the day was that Joel was nowhere to be seen. He must be out sick today, Pixie thought. English class would be better without him there, but she forgot that she had to bring something in to talk about to class today. How could she be so forgetful about her schoolwork?

"I'm sorry, Miss Peters. I completely forgot to bring my item in today," Pixie told her teacher.

"Pixie, that's unlike you to forget an assignment. I will have to take fifteen points off to start and you will have to share it with the class tomorrow," her teacher said.

"OK, Miss Peters. Thank you." This was turning out to be a bad day. All Pixie wanted to do was crawl under her covers and hide.

The end of the day was finally approaching, which meant gym class. She didn't understand why her school had gym every day when most schools had it every other day. Especially on this day when all she wanted was another study hall to fall asleep in.

"Alright, girls, five laps around the gym. Miss Willow, what's with the hat? You must take it off," said Miss Webb.

"I would prefer to keep it on if it's OK," Cinda said.

"I'm sorry, Miss Willow, not in gym class." Cinda looked at Pixie and slowly took her hat off with tears in her eyes. Gasps were heard from the girls around Tantra.

"What in the world did you do to your hair? Was that on purpose? It looks really bad," said Tantra.

"I guess pink's the new blond," said Samantha as the two laughed.

"Alright, everyone, that's enough. Do your five laps. Miss Willow, I'd like to speak to you, please."

Pixie and the rest of the class ran laps as Miss Webb talked to Cinda. Pixie wondered what they were saying when Tantra passed her and it looked like she was flying above the floor. Pixie guessed everyone was wondering about Cinda's hair and hadn't even noticed Tantra. She hoped Lillian could fix things because she didn't know what else to do. Class finally ended and everyone headed to the locker room. Pixie couldn't wait to get home.

Cinda was already on the bus, sitting in the back and looking out the window. Pixie sat next to her and noticed Cinda was still in her gym clothes. "Are you alright?" asked Pixie. "What did Miss Webb say to you?"

"She wanted to know why I did this to my hair," Cinda said. "I told her I made a mistake with the color. She believed me. I guess it doesn't matter now; everyone will know about it since Tantra has seen it."

"If it's any consolation, while we were running around doing our laps Tantra was off the ground the whole time." Cinda slowly turned and looked at Pixie as they both laughed.

Chapter 10

Mad Friends
& Bad Enemies

$\mathcal{P}$ixie piled up her books for school, putting them into her backpack. She decided that since she had finished her homework early she would read the final three chapters in the Opish book. She was determined to make it back to the House of Charms to help both Cinda and Tantra with their problems before they got worse. She might even be able to help herself with those bad dreams. So far it seemed that Tantra was unaware of her flying abilities; thank goodness no one else noticed either.

Opening the book to Chapter Seven, Pixie repeated the title a few times, finally making the ops float off the page to reveal the words, "Arranging Environment." As she read through the chapter, she learned that a living space had to be circular to blend in with the environment. Anything added such as huts, plants or trees had to stay true to the natural environment. The living area had to be unnoticeable, just in case outsiders happened to stroll through. The chapter went on to talk about the plants, butterflies, bugs and animals that should be encouraged to live in the area to create the perfect blend of nature.

Pixie finished the chapter in no time. Looking up from the book she thought about what she had just read. It sounded like some kind of secret society, people living together in a compound afraid of being found. It made Pixie sad to think of how frightened they must have been. Pixie thought about her dream and about how the people may have been found by the outside world and destroyed for their differences. How sad, she thought.

Checking the time, Pixie realized she could easily finish the last two chapters in the book before her mom knocked on her door to remind her it was time for bed. She turned to Chapter Eight, "Blending into the Background." This consisted of thinking positive thoughts relating to peace and love. A calm mind meant a calm body, one that could become invisible to the outside world. Common practices of meditation and t'ai chi were required among the group. Love and kindness toward everything -- the environment, animals and one another -- would create an aura that would actually make people disappear. It sounded impossible; how could one disappear with love and kindness? Pixie had so many questions that needed to be answered. She decided to take out her journal and make a list of questions along with a summary of each chapter so when she met with Lillian P. Moss she would be prepared.

Pixie turned to the last chapter: "Kopeepopioping Sopecropeats," translated to "Keeping Secrets." She slowly read the last few pages:

"Now that you have come to the end you have probably figured out that we are not like everyone else. We are from a different race. Yes, we are human; you could say we have a unique nationality unknown to others or thought of as make believe by the majority of people. We have special talents; we can do different things that would make it hard for others to accept us as normal. With this knowledge we must keep our qualities secret if we are to blend in with the rest of the human race. If we want to live a life outside of the circle, outside of the woods amongst others different from ourselves we must keep our secrets for the sake of our survival. Please be thoughtful. We don't want to be hunted down, leading us to extinction by others who may not understand or find us unacceptable. Always share love and kindness to all living beings inside and outside of the circle. Signing off in a loving way hoping we will always be, Please keep the secret… Lillian P. Moss 1883"

Pixie shut the book. Staring down at it in disbelief, she wondered if it could actually be true that Lillian would have been around in 1883. No, Pixie thought. That would make her more than 100 years old. She was old but not that old. It had to be someone else. Yes, that's it, her grandmother or something. This made more sense; Lillian was not the author but was related to the author.

A knock at the door startled Pixie. "I'll be right there," she said as she got up to put the book away.

"It's Mom. Can I come in? I'd like to talk to you about something unusual that's happened."

Pixie opened her door to let her mom in. "What is it, Mom? You sound worried."

"Well, yes. I was talking to Cinda's mom earlier today and she told me about Cinda's hair turning pink and how impossible it is to wash it out. Do you know anything about this?"

"Why would I know? I think it's odd, too. I'm not sure why it happened. I did try to cheer Cinda up by telling her that at least it's her favorite color, but that didn't go over well."

"We're concerned about you girls; I hope you're not getting involved in something you shouldn't."

"Like what?" asked Pixie.

"I don't know. I was hoping you would tell me."

"Well, nothing that I know of that would do that to Cinda's hair."

"I want you to know, Pixie, that you can tell me anything," her mother said. "I want you to feel comfortable enough to share your thoughts on whatever; just know I'm here to help."

"Thanks, Mom. That means a lot. I will share with you when there's something interesting to share."

"OK, agreed. Why don't you get ready for bed now; school's tomorrow."

"That sounds like a good idea." Pixie kissed her mom goodnight and headed into the bathroom to brush her teeth. Pixie's mom walked over to the door of Pixie's room and stood for a moment, lost in thought, until she decided to go to bed herself.

Pixie jumped into bed. Her journal was by her pillow and she picked it up to add, "I think Cinda, Tantra, and myself all are from some secret society that had special qualities, maybe magical powers." Pixie put her journal down, thinking that now she would have to carry it with her at all times because her mom was onto what was happening.

Pixie wanted to talk to her mom about it, but she wanted to find out more before she did. She didn't want to be told not to continue with her exploration. Plus she had to go back to help Cinda and Tantra with their problems. Pixie thought about her next trip out to the House of Charms now that she had finished the book. She would probably have to go alone this time.

Getting sleepy, Pixie shut her light off and lay down. As she slowly drifted off her thoughts were brought back to the fires and the three girls running for their lives, running to the House of Charms and up to the front door where Lillian P. Moss welcomed them.

Pixie shot up out of bed. Lillian was there; she was there when this terrible thing happened. When did it happen? Why? Pixie tried to go back to sleep but couldn't get the dream out of her mind. Another sleepless night, she thought.

Pixie was lying in bed with her eyes open as she listened to the sounds of the night turn into morning. The birds started chirping outside her window as daylight peeked through the sky. She knew that she would have to get up soon for school. Getting no sleep two nights in a row made her extremely tired this morning.

While packing her books for school, Pixie also stuck her journal inside her backpack. She felt confident enough about the Opish book not being found since her mom knew nothing about the loose floorboard. She would have put the journal in there too but there wasn't enough room.

Pixie's dad knocked on her door and looked in. "Wow, you're up and ready to go this morning. What's the special occasion?"

"I couldn't sleep last night so I just decided to get ready for school early instead of lying in bed with my eyes open."

"Anything going on that you want to talk about? School going good?"

"Everything is fine, Dad. I'm just having a hard time sleeping lately."

"You're not stressed about something? Sometimes stress can cause insomnia."

"Nope, not stressed."

"That's good. Since you're up, come down and join me for breakfast. Mom's making us scrambled eggs and toast."

"Sounds good, I'll be right down," said Pixie.

Pixie carried her backpack downstairs, following her dad to the kitchen. "Pixie, you're ready to go already? You still have an hour before the bus arrives," said Mrs. Elm as she watched her daughter carefully.

"I know, I just can't get to sleep at all lately so I decided to get ready for school instead. Why prolong the agony?" Pixie said.

All three sat quietly as they began eating breakfast. The only sounds were the clanking of teacups on saucers, butter and jam spreading on toast, and the shuffling of newspaper as her dad turned the pages. Pixie could feel her mom looking at her the whole time. She focused on her breakfast, trying to hurry so she could break away from the silence.

"I guess I'll wait outside for the bus; I need the fresh air to get me started today," Pixie said.

"I'm on my way out soon too, so I'll see you before you leave," her dad said, still reading the paper.

"I made a lunch for you this morning, here it is," said Mrs. Elm as she handed Pixie a bag and kissed her on the forehead. "Love you."

"Love you too, Mom."

Pixie left the house thinking about how weird her mom was acting this morning. She definitely had to know something was up; Pixie just hoped she hadn't guessed what it was. She stood outside for a while waiting for Cinda to join her, and she noticed her dad leaving the house to go to work. Driving by, he rolled down the window and said, "See you later, kid. Have fun in school today."

"I will, Dad," Pixie said, rolling her eyes and waving as he drove away.

Cinda made it out of her house just in time as the bus came up to the driveway. She had a wool hat on, leading Pixie to believe that her hair was still pink. Pixie turned to notice Tantra opening her front door and walking out to the bus stop with no skateboard this morning. How odd, she thought. Tantra never left the house without her skateboard. Not having time to talk to either of them, Pixie stepped onto the bus and the girls sat in separate seats. Pixie could tell Cinda wanted to be left alone.

The bus ride was a long one, and Pixie couldn't wait for the day to be over. She had a feeling it might be filled with trouble.

Pixie ran into Carl on her way to homeroom and they talked about the paper. "I still can't believe you didn't get editor in chief," Carl said. "You should have been it this year, just like the other two years. You definitely have more experience than what's-his-name, Mr. California."

"His name is Zeb, Carl, and I'm fine with it. Zeb will do great, I'm sure of it. Besides, we're there to help out."

"I'm not sure I want to help make him look good."

"Carl, you're being silly."

The two entered homeroom and took their seats. Joel was already seated behind Pixie's desk. She checked her seat before sitting down to make sure he hadn't done anything stupid.

"Oh, how cute, the lovebirds have arrived. What are you two talking about today? Which one is smarter

115

than the other? Or are you discussing a math problem? Which is it?" asked Joel, leaning toward them as his friends laughed.

"Joel, why don't you just give it up already. You're not even funny; it's so sad to listen to you try," Pixie said as she turned back in her seat. Joel had no time to reply as the bell went off. Later Pixie left with Carl, tossing her backpack over her shoulder.

"I get so mad when he's around. He's always trying to pick on me about something," Pixie said.

"Yeah, he's a real jerk; pay no attention to him. I sometimes think it's his way of flirting with you."

"Carl, please. Joel hates me for some reason; maybe I intimidate him."

"That could be, but I think he's flirting; he is childish like that."

"I'll see you later," said Pixie as she shook her head at Carl and walked into her biology class.

Zeb was already at the lab table reading up on their next experiment. "Hey, Pixie, how's it going?" he asked, looking up from his book.

"Great, now. What are you doing?"

"Just starting our assignment so we can maybe finish early."

"Great idea."

Mrs. Stevens walked in, quieting the class and passing out equipment for the project. "Alright, everyone, try to get through as much as you can today. You will have another day to finish up if you don't get done today."

"Attention, attention, students of Cedar High! Special announcement." Everyone looked up as they listened to a voice that sounded like Joel's on the loudspeaker.

In the background a teacher shouted, "Mr. Emerson, give me that intercom this minute."

The sound of the teacher chasing Joel could be heard as Joel continued: "I have some important information that I received this morning. Ahem," Joel cleared his throat. "I have acquired information that Pixie, Cinda and Tantra have special qualities, such as magical powers. This information comes from a green journal I received in homeroom this morning from the author, Pixie Elm. So beware, students; they could put a spell on you." Before Joel could say any more a muffled sound was heard as the teacher finally grabbed the intercom away.

Pixie's entire biology class turned and stared at her and started laughing. In a fury, Pixie grabbed her backpack and searched for her journal. It wasn't there. Did Joel steal it or had it fallen out? She didn't know. All she knew was that she was crying while she put her books in her backpack.

"Alright, class, settle down," said Mrs. Stevens. "It's time to get back to work."

Zeb looked mad as Pixie left the class crying. Pixie hoped that he wasn't mad at her for leaving him to do all the work on their lab assignment as she made her way under the staircase to hide and collect her thoughts. How could this have happened? She was so careful about everything. Did Joel read all of it? Did he find out more than he had time to say? Thanks to the teacher who had grabbed him, he didn't say any more. Oh, no, what about Cinda and Tantra? They are probably so angry right now, Pixie thought, and she wouldn't blame them, either. All she wished right now was to be a speck of dust on the floor where no one would notice her. I have to be strong and act like this was nothing, that Joel was being his stupid self and all will be forgotten, she thought.

Pixie could hear people talking and laughing about the announcement as they walked through the halls. She waited a little while longer under the staircase, when suddenly she heard Joel talking with two of his friends. "That was classic, Joel. Where did you come up with that?" asked one of them.

"Pixie's journal fell out of her backpack and landed on my desk; how could I not read it?"

"Where is it now?" asked Pete.

"I'm not sure; I think in the office. There was nothing else interesting in it."

"Did you get detention?"

"Yeah, after school two days, but it was worth it."

"Hey, Joel!" Pixie heard a voice yell. It sounded like Zeb. "Joel, why are you such an idiot? Don't you have anything better to do than pick on nice girls."

"Listen, what's your name -- Zip, Zap, I can't remember, not that I care," said Joel as his friends laughed.

"It's Zeb, and I'm tired of your stupid behavior just to get a laugh; you're not funny." A crowd started to form around Joel as he took a leap at Zeb and began punching him. Zeb fought back as the two fell to the floor and the crowd cheered.

"Break it up, break it up. What's going on here? That's enough," said Mr. Jackson as he and another teacher separated the two boys. The teachers sent the two to the office as the rest of the students booed.

"Everyone get to class now!" yelled Mr. Beech, who was escorting Zeb to the office followed by Mr. Jackson bringing Joel.

Pixie decided it was time to sneak out and head to math class. She couldn't stop going to her classes because of all of this. She loved Zeb for standing up for her. Hopefully he wouldn't get into too much trouble.

As Pixie entered math class she could feel the stares. A few girls were whispering and laughing as she sat down. She knew it would be something she would have to deal with in every class; she thought she might as well face it now instead of prolonging the agony.

Mr. Jackson entered, probably having just left the office where he dropped off Joel. "Alright, now, it's been an eventful day. Things were said as a prank that should now be forgotten, so let's get back to math. I hope everyone is prepared today; I thought a surprise quiz would be a perfect start."

The class groaned. "When you're finished please hand them up to me and sit quietly so the rest of the students can finish," Mr. Jackson said.

Pixie was one of the first students to hand in her paper. As she placed it on Mr. Jackson's desk he looked up at her from his plan book. "Miss Elm, I think I have something of yours," he said as he reached into his carry case and took out a green sparkly journal. "Is this your journal?"

"Yes, it is, Mr. Jackson."

"I think you should be more aware of your personal belongings next time. The office noted that your journal is completely empty, so it looks like Joel has played a practical joke on you." Mr. Jackson spoke loud enough for the class to hear. "This could be a good story for the newspaper to help clear things up."

"That sounds like a great idea, Mr. Jackson," Pixie said.

Pixie took her journal back to her desk. She flipped it open and noticed that Mr. Jackson was right: Everything she had written had disappeared. It was so odd; she wished she could share this with someone. A journal that makes what you've written disappear if anyone else gets hold of it. How great was that! Maybe Joel only saw the last entry; the rest must have disappeared as he opened it. What was happening here? Pixie needed to find out soon; she couldn't handle another weird thing in her life.

The classes went smoother than she thought they would. Word got out that Pixie's journal had been empty and that Joel was just being Joel. Pixie was happy about that. She didn't feel so bad about what happened anymore, until she went to lunch.

"Pixie, are you alright?" asked Jane as she caught up to her entering the cafeteria.

"Yes, I'm fine. Joel was trying to be funny by humiliating me in front of everyone."

Just then a student in the cafeteria played "Black Magic Woman" on his iPod speakers as she walked in. Everyone laughed and made jokes. "Put a spell on me," shouted someone in the cafeteria.

"Come on, Pixie, let's go outside for lunch today," Jane said. Molly and Carl spotted them taking their lunch outside and followed.

Just then Pixie heard footsteps coming up from behind her. "I don't know what you were thinking when you wrote that. How could you bring your journal to school? What a stupid thing to do."

Pixie turned around and was face to face with Cinda. "Cinda, I didn't do anything to hurt you; my journal is completely empty." Pixie took it out to show her. Cinda grabbed it and threw it on the ground.

"I don't want to hear it. People are looking at me like I'm some kind of a weirdo. Look at my hair!" Cinda pulled her hat off and Molly and Jane gasped. "It's all pink and I can't get it out. I'm a complete wreck and you just made it worse."

"Cinda, I'm sorry. I'll find a way to fix things."

"Whatever," said Cinda as she turned and walked away.

"Wow, I've never seen Cinda so mad. She really believes you wrote that," said Carl.

"Yeah, well, that's nothing. I have a feeling Tantra won't be that nice," said Pixie.

"I forgot about that. I haven't seen her at all today," said Jane.

"We do have gym with her last period; that should be fun," said Molly.

Pixie picked up her journal as they headed to a picnic table. "She's in my woodworking class right after lunch so I'm sure she can't wait to talk to me."

Pixie listened to her friends talk as her thoughts started to wander. She was thinking about how it felt walking the hallways with everyone staring and laughing at her. She could just imagine Cinda and Tantra facing the same thing, all because of her stupidity. Pixie now felt she definitely had to make it up to them by making a trip back to the House of Charms as soon as possible. Lillian could help Cinda with her pink hair and Tantra with her flying, she just knew it.

"Pixie, are you coming?" asked Jane.

"What? What happened?" Pixie asked.

"The bell rang; it's time for us to get to our next class. Are you alright?" Carl said.

"I'm fine. Just thinking, that's all." Pixie got up and headed to her next class and the dreaded confrontation with Tantra.

She tried to walk as slowly as possible, hoping to enter class just as the bell rang. Pixie was just about to walk in when someone grabbed her by the arm and dragged her to a hidden doorway.

"What are you doing?" said Pixie, startled as she turned and saw it was Tantra who was now standing face to face with her.

"Tantra, I'm really sorry for what I've done. It was stupid of me to bring my journal to class. If it means anything at all my journal was completely empty except for what Joel read, which wasn't much."

"Stop! Stop this talk right now and let me speak," said Tantra as her face turned red. "You're so lucky I can't take care of you right now, because if I could I would knock you flat out. I just noticed that my anger has brought on a strange problem, however: Every time I want to knock you out I rise off the ground." As Tantra said this, she levitated a good six inches.

"Oh, my! I'm so sorry, Tantra. I didn't mean for this to happen."

"Yeah, well, it has, and it's all from that crazy place we went to. How did I let you talk me into it? How stupid you are to write about it and bring it to school and have Joel of all people find it."

"I know; it's not my best decision. Has anyone seen you like this?" Pixie asked as she looked at Tantra still hovering above the ground.

"No, are you kidding? As soon as it started I hid in the bathroom. I'm leaving for home after this pleasant conversation."

"Well, stop being angry so you can walk out of here," Pixie said.

"Oh, I would just like to get my hands on you right now. People have been looking at me like I'm some kind of a weirdo." Tantra rose higher each time her anger increased. "No one has looked at me that way before; I'm not used to it like you."

"Tantra, please calm down. I want to help you," Pixie said.

"Oh, yeah? How come nothing has happened to you?"

"It has. I can't sleep at night, I've been having horrible dreams."

"Oh, poor you. I feel sorry for you," Tantra mocked.

"I'm going to find a way to fix our problems," said Pixie.

"You better, because I refuse to live like this." With that Tantra slowly lowered to the ground, walking away from Pixie as she sneaked out of school with a friend's skateboard.

Pixie watched her go. As soon as Tantra was far enough away she got on the skateboard and started down the street. Pixie watched as Tantra began to fly up from the street through the woods. There had to be a cure for these things, Pixie thought. Lillian P. Moss would know what to do.

Chapter 11

Secret Remedies

Pixie stared at her ceiling after another sleepless night. Today was a new day. She knew that she would have to take care of the mess and stop Cinda and Tantra from hating her. It would have to be after school; she would make another trip to the House of Charms to find a cure.

Pixie wished she was a person who could just forget about things and go on with her life without meddling with something that should be left alone. But that wasn't her; she had to finish it. She needed to find out what it all meant.

As Pixie headed out the door to catch the bus she realized that both Cinda and Tantra weren't going to school. She wanted to hide before the bus came but it was too late. There she was, alone, boarding the bus with a few classmates on it already. She could feel everyone staring at her like she was from another planet, and at that moment she felt like she was.

The bus stopped at school and Pixie jumped off and headed straight for the nurse's office. She couldn't handle another day of school, not as tired as she was. She hoped her mom wouldn't mind picking her up.

Walking into the nurse's office was a new experience for Pixie, as she would never think of missing a day of school. There were only a few times when she was so sick that her mom made her stay in bed.

"May I help you?" asked an old woman with large glasses sitting behind a desk as Pixie walked in.

"Yes, I just got off the bus and I feel very sick to my stomach. I'm starting to feel dizzy too."

"Have a seat against the wall; the nurse will see you shortly."

Pixie looked over at the seats by the wall, where she saw Tom, a cute guy with short, dark, curly hair. His leg was cut, and dried blood was forming around a badly applied bandage. Pixie hated to lie about being sick; she hoped she'd be able to pull it off.

The nurse came out with a boy who was walking with his head down. "I'm sorry, your temperature is normal; there is nothing wrong with you that I can tell. I suppose you should go to homeroom. Bye, now," the nurse said. The boy left with a disappointed look.

He probably has a test that he forgot to study for, Pixie thought.

"Oh, Tom, what happened this time?" asked the nurse, an attractive, dark-haired woman with a tanned complexion. She would give Snow White a run for her money in the niceness department.

"I fell off the bus and cut my leg. The bus driver tried to bandage me up," Tom said.

"Let's take a look at it. I'll have it fixed up in no time." The nurse took Tom into the room to redo the bandage.

After the bell for homeroom rang, the nurse came out with Tom, who was freshly bandaged.

"Whom do we have here?" she asked as she looked at Pixie.

"Um, my name is Pixie."

"I've never seen you here before; are you new to school?"

"No, I've just never been to the nurse's office before."

"Well, come on in; let's see how you're doing."

Pixie followed the nurse and took a seat on the cot.

"Alright, Pixie, how are you feeling?" Miss Hawthorn asked.

"Not too good. I feel sick; I think I may throw up. I'm not sure why. It just came on suddenly. I'm feeling dizzy too."

"Well, you don't seem like the type to put on a story. Why don't we call someone to pick you up? I think you'll be fine after some rest; you look tired. Drink plenty of liquids, and try some chicken noodle soup."

"I will, Miss Hawthorn," Pixie said as the nurse called Pixie's mom to pick her up.

When Mrs. Elm arrived at the school she said, "Alright Pixie, let's get home and get you straight to bed."

"Jill, is that you?" asked the nurse.

"Oh, my, Holly. How are you? It's been such a long time."

"It has; we need to get together sometime and catch up," Miss Hawthorn said.

"I would love that, Holly. How about sometime this weekend? Dana would love to see you as well."

"That would be great; here's my number."

"Call you tomorrow. Bye, Holly."

"Yes, see you. Take care, Pixie."

Pixie waved at Miss Hawthorn as she followed her mom to the car. "Mom, how do you know the school nurse?"

"We've been friends since we were young girls."

"Cinda's mom knows her too?"

"Yes. When Dana came to visit her dad over the summer the three of us would hang out all the time, like peas in a pod."

"I learn something new about you every day," said Pixie.

"What does that mean? I don't have any secrets, Pixie."

"I know, Mom."

The two finished the ride home in silence. As they entered the house Pixie's mom said, "I suggest you go up to bed. I'll get you a cup of tea."

Pixie couldn't wait to get upstairs and figure out a way to get to the House of Charms. Throwing her backpack to the side she noticed her cell phone had a message on it. It read: "I need help, I can't leave room, can't stop flying."

Tantra was in trouble. Pixie had to help her today. She texted back that she was on her way, hoping there was some way she could sneak out.

Pixie put on her sleep shirt and kept on the rest of her clothes. She got herself into bed just in time as her mom entered the room with tea.

"Pixie, here is your tea. I want you to stay in bed for now. There is some soup downstairs; just heat it up, OK? I have to go to the flower shop, so please stay in bed and do some homework."

"I will, Mom. Thanks for the tea."

"Alright, I'll be home around three. Love you."

"Love you too, Mom."

127

As soon as Pixie heard her mom leave she was up and out of bed, changing her shirt and packing her backpack with the Opish book. She threw her bag over her shoulder, ran downstairs through the kitchen and out the back door, jumping off the porch to make her way to Tantra's house.

Pixie stood under Tantra's window as she picked up a pebble and tossed it to get her attention. Tantra opened the window and looked out.

"Are you OK?" Pixie said.

"No, I'm not. I've been flying around my room all day. It stopped for a while when my parents came in to check on me. I can't go to school like this; people will think I'm a freak. I'm not sure how to control it."

"I'm going to the House of Charms right now; maybe you can go with me. Lillian might be able to help you."

"No, I'm not going back there. That woman has done enough to me already."

"Maybe this is a sign for you to stop fighting what we might be," Pixie said.

"Oh, please; don't start this again."

"Then why did you call me? I'm only trying to help."

"You're the only one who wouldn't think I'm crazy when I told you I'm flying because you're just as crazy."

"Well, I'm going to the House of Charms," Pixie said. "I'll see what I can do for you; maybe there is something I can buy at the store for this."

"I'm sure there is. That's probably why this is happening. She had no customers until three stupid girls walked in the door that night. She'll probably try to sell you the whole shop."

"I'll be on the lookout for that," Pixie said. "I'll stop by when I get back."

As Pixie left, Tantra started to fly around her room again. Grabbing onto her headboard, she pulled herself under her bed.

Pixie headed off into the woods, running as fast as she could and crossing over the small bridge. She followed the butterfly wings up on the trees.

Pixie had to get to the House of Charms as soon as possible; she needed to help Cinda and Tantra and herself. As she followed the trees through the woods she came across the dead circle in the forest. Pixie thought for the first time about the fires in her dream; could this be where that terrible night took place? Walking through the circle she started to feel the fear from many years before. The fear those poor people must have felt losing their home and their lives. Pixie quickly ran across to the other side of the forest, making her way to the small house in the back of the woods.

She stood by the large boulder and looked at the House of Charms. The chimney was smoking, a sign that someone must be home. Pixie walked up to the front door and knocked. As she did the door opened by itself.

"Hello, Lillian? Noon? It's me, Pixie. I've come back with the Opish book. I finished it. Is anyone here?" Pixie slowly entered and decided to call up the stairs to the library, remembering that Lillian had a hard time hearing. "Lillian, are you up there?"

"Who's there?" answered Lillian.

"It's me, Pixie. I've finished the Opish book. You told me to come back when I've read through it."

"Oh, yes. I'll be right down." Lillian slowly made her way down the stairs, wearing her robes and the strange necklace with the stones missing.

"How are you, dear? Have you girls finished with the Opish book already?" Lillian asked.

"I'm the only one who read the book; my friends didn't have time with schoolwork and all."

"Oh, yes," said Lillian. "They haven't come around yet. They will, though. They will. So, Pixie, what do you think about what you've read?"

"I had problems with the Opish language but I figured it out. I'm not able to speak it fluently, though."

"That comes in time. At least you understand the language."

"I feel like I can create a small woodland village now from the information in the book," Pixie said.

"Very good, very good. Come join me upstairs in my library so we can sit and talk about what you've learned."

Just as Pixie started to follow Lillian up the stairs, Noon entered through the back door.

"Hey, Pixie, how are you?" he asked.

"Fine, Noon. It's nice to see you again."

"Are your friends here too?"

"No, just me. I've come to return the Opish book and talk to Lillian."

"Well, I'll be downstairs keeping the fire going; come visit me when you're done," Noon said.

"Thanks, I will," said Pixie.

Pixie headed up the stairs where Lillian was already seated at a small square table in the middle of a room surrounded by bookshelves. All the books seemed to sparkle just like the Opish book. Lillian had her face in one, holding a magnifying glass to her eye. She looked up at Pixie and laughed. "The print is so small in this book I need one of these."

Pixie nodded. "What's next," she asked. "Is there anything else I should know?"

"No, now it's time that you feel what's next," Lillian said.

"I may be feeling it already; I've been having some bad dreams about fires, people losing their homes and their lives. I wanted to ask you if these dreams are real."

Lillian looked nervous, not knowing what to say. She had no idea that Pixie would see into the past so soon. "It sounds like you're having dreams about events that happened in the past. I would like to tell you more but I'm not sure it's the right time yet for that," she said.

"I saw you in my dreams," Pixie said. "Three young girls escaped the fires and ran to you here at the House of Charms."

"Yes, that did happen. I can't tell you what it all means. Not yet, anyway."

"The dead circle in the forest, is that where the fire took place?"

"Yes, it was," said Lillian.

"This Opish book has a passage at the end and the name that is signed at the bottom is yours. Isn't this book old? I mean real old, like sometime in the 1800s. How could that be? Were you alive back then?"

"Again, I can explain all that when you are able to feel what's been hidden for so many years. So many have hidden this feeling that our uniqueness is leaving and will no longer be a part of future generations. You girls must bring back the power that we have hidden for so many years."

"How do we do that?" asked Pixie.

"You must be in tune with nature," Lillian said. "See the beauty in all things. Live like you will always be young. Hold onto that youthfulness that sometimes slips away when we get older. Find your passion. We have something special that others don't have or understand. We need to share these things so people will accept us."

"How are we so different from others? We look the same. I thought we may have lived in communes and that is what made us different," Pixie said.

"That is true; we did live that way. Some may still in other parts of the world but there is much more to it than that. Like I've said before, I just don't think you're there yet. You need to feel it more to understand. I will say you are close, though."

"Lillian, I have to ask you something before I forget."

"What's that, my dear?"

"My friend Tantra, she was here with me on our first visit. Well, she has this problem now. She can't seem to stop flying around her house."

"Oh, yes." Lillian laughed. "Those things do happen sometimes."

"Is there something I can give her to make it stop?"

"It seems our hidden secrets that were bottled up for so long have had the lid come off since you girls came to visit. When Tantra stops fighting the fact that she is different from others, she will be able to control this."

"I don't see that happening anytime soon," Pixie said. "Is there anything I can give her to fix it now?"

"Maybe you can give her this," Lillian said as she got up from her chair and put her wooden-framed glasses down. She led Pixie downstairs to the store.

Lillian handed Pixie two river rocks. "What do I tell her to do with these?" Pixie asked.

"Oh, yes. Well, let's see." Pixie thought Lillian seemed to be making it up as she went along and she started to have doubts about the remedy. "Tell her to hit the rocks together three times in the morning and again three times at night like this." Lillian struck them together, causing a gold sparkly dust to fly around. "This will stop it from happening."

"This will work?" asked Pixie, still not convinced.

"Yes, yes it will," said Lillian, smiling. Lillian dropped the rocks into Pixie's hand.

"OK, how about this one," asked Pixie. "My friend Cinda, her hair has turned pink and it won't wash out. She woke up one morning to pink hair, and the color seems to get brighter each day."

"Pink, you say?" asked Lillian. She was now deep in thought. "Of course it would be pink." Pixie looked at Lillian doubtfully. "Oh, yes, take this feather. Have her put it under her pillow when she sleeps, always remembering to hide it when she wakes."

Pixie put all of the items in her backpack. "Thanks, Lillian. I'll give these to the girls."

"Well?"

"Well what?" asked Pixie.

"What about you? Do you need something or are you fine?"

"I'm just having those dreams that keep me up all night," Pixie said.

"I want you to know it's nothing for you to fear, except that it is your right to know. I'm sure you will be able to sleep better now," Lillian said.

"Alright, I'll try that. Thanks, Lillian."

"I'm very tired now; I'm an old woman, you know. I need my sleep. Come back again."

"I will. Thanks for everything" said Pixie.

Lillian slowly walked to a door under the steps and entered her small room to sleep.

Pixie wanted to see Noon before she left. She walked down the back hall and knocked on his door, which was open enough to see him inside with his blue chalk in hand and candles lit. "Hi, Pixie, come in," he said.

"Wow, Noon, your pictures are beautiful."

"Thanks. I love to draw; I guess, it's my passion." Noon smiled at Pixie.

"It must be. Noon, I forgot to pay Lillian for the items she gave me from the shop."

"Those items are free; we don't charge anyone for something that comes from nature. It's a gift to cherish. A reminder to not forget nature and all its beautiful things."

"I see. Well, please thank Lillian for me. I should get back before my parents get home; they don't know that I left."

"Sure. Oh, wait." Noon walked over to one of his drawings and rolled it up before handing it to Pixie. "Can you give this to Cinda, please? Tell her I said hi and would love to see her again."

"I will," Pixie said. "See you, Noon."

As soon as Pixie left the house she took off running through the woods back to Tantra's house to give her the rocks, hoping it would help.

Pixie threw some pebbles at Tantra's window again. Tantra opened the window, but she seemed to be upside down.

"Tantra, are you OK?"

"Oh, yeah, just fine," Tantra said sarcastically. "Look at me; what do you think?"

"I have something to help you with that, but I guess you can't come downstairs to get it."

"That's not happening. I've been flying around all day. How can I get downstairs like this?"

"I don't know. Fly, maybe?"

"Real funny," Tantra said. "There's a ladder in the backyard. Just pull the latch up to open the gate and bring it here quietly. My mom is still home, I don't want her to know what's going on."

Pixie got the ladder, trying not to make any noise. It was heavy but she got it up to Tantra's window without a sound. Pixie climbed up and looked inside. "Wow, that looks like fun," she said.

"Yeah, lots of fun. If I could control it it would be."

"Here, Lillian gave me these to give to you." Pixie pulled out the river rocks from her backpack.

"What's that? A couple of rocks, are you kidding? How much did you pay for that hoax?"

"It was free. Everything in the store is free because it's all a part of nature."

"What do I do with them?"

"You have to hit them together three times in the morning and three times at night. I'm sure it will still work if you do it now."

"This is silly, but I'll do it just to humor you."

Pixie was unsure about it too. She hoped Lillian was right.

Tantra took the rocks and hit them together three times. Gold dust sparkled around Tantra's purple room. Then nothing happened. Pixie looked scared as Tantra stared at her, still in the air with evil in her eyes. Then, all of a sudden, "thud!" Tantra fell to the ground. Pixie gasped. Tantra stood up and walked around her room, smiling.

"Tantra are you OK?" called Mrs. Birch from below. Pixie heard her coming up the stairs and she quickly headed down the ladder and returned it to the side of the gate. She could hear Mrs. Birch ask Tantra again, "Are you OK? What happened?"

"Nothing, Mom. I'm fine, see?"

Pixie headed over to Cinda's house next, hoping she would let her in. She knocked on the front door and waited till it finally opened.

"Good afternoon, Pixie. Did you stay home from school today too?"

"It's nice to see you, Grandpa Willow. Yes, I left school not feeling well. I wanted to drop off some homework for Cinda before I forgot."

"Oh, sure thing; come on in. Would you like some mint tea? I'm making myself a cup."

"No, thanks; I'm fine."

"Cinda is up in her room. You know, you girls need to be careful about things you don't understand fully. I'm here to help if you want it."

"OK. Thanks, Grandpa Willow." Pixie almost felt as if Cinda's grandpa knew that they went to the House of Charms and that crazy things had happened. She guessed Cinda's pink hair was a giveaway. Maybe we should talk to him; he might be able to tell us what it's all about, she thought. Could he keep a secret, though?

Pixie knocked on Cinda's bedroom door.

"Who is it?" Cinda said.

"It's me, Pixie."

"Go away."

"I have something for you that will help with your hair."

"I said go away."

"I also have a picture that Noon wanted me to give to you that he drew."

Cinda came to the door and opened it. "He did? Where is it?"

Pixie pulled the picture out of her backpack along with the feather. "Here it is," she said as she handed the rolled up picture to Cinda, who grabbed it and opened it carefully. Both of them looked down at it in shock.

136

"That's you, Cinda! Noon drew a picture of you."

"It is," said Cinda.

The picture sparkled blue and seemed to radiate off the page. "It's so good; he's a great artist," said Cinda.

"He is. I think you may need to hide it from your parents, though. How will you explain the glow?"

"You're right. I'll put it in my closet. Do you think he may like me?" asked Cinda.

"I would have to guess yes."

"You went to the House of Charms today? Why didn't you go to school? You hardly ever miss a day in your life," said Cinda.

"I did go to school but you and Tantra weren't there and I knew I needed to get help for the both of you soon. So I went to the nurse's office and had my mom pick me up. As soon as my mom left for work I snuck out to the House of Charms. Here is a feather that Lillian gave me. She said to put it under your pillow when you sleep, but hide it when you wake. I'd do it every day just to be on the safe side."

"I feel crazy saying this but I'm going to miss my pink hair. I kind of stood out," Cinda said.

"That you did."

"I can't wait to try this out to see if it works."

"I have a feeling it will," Pixie said. "Lillian gave me rocks for Tantra to use to make her stop flying and it worked."

"Did Tantra let you in her room?"

"No, I had to climb a ladder to her window."

"I can't believe she listened to you," Cinda said.

"She was desperate," said Pixie. "What time is it?"

"It's just two o'clock," said Cinda.

137

"I should get back home before my mom does. She thinks I'm in bed resting."

"Pixie, the next time you go to the House of Charms I might want to go with you. I'd like to see Noon again," Cinda said.

"That would be great," said Pixie. "I'll see you tomorrow." Pixie left, hoping Cinda would really go back with her to the House of Charms. As she walked home she tried to zip up her backpack when an envelope fell out. It was addressed to her. She opened it and read the letter inside as she walked into her house:

Dearest Pixie,

Find the emerald stone. It is your family stone; it has been lost for many years. I believe it wants to be found now. Check the secret hallway; you should find it in there. When you do, bring it back to me.

Yours truly,

Lillian P. Moss

When did she leave this with me? I didn't even see her drop it in my bag, Pixie thought. Could the secret hallway be the one she found under the auditorium? The emerald stone. Her stone. Now she couldn't wait to get back to school. She needed to find this emerald stone.

Chapter 12

Finding the Emerald Stone

Pixie was alone in her room, looking up at the ceiling and thinking about the emerald stone. The Opish book had mentioned different stones and the meanings behind each one, and Pixie had picked out a stone for her, Cinda, Tantra, and even Noon and Lillian. Could she have been right about the stones matching with the right person? She did see herself in the emerald stone. Lillian had called it her family stone.

As Pixie looked around her room she noticed something she hadn't thought too much about before: Her room was green, her favorite color. She also had found her favorite journal at a garage sale and it had seemed to call out to her, all sparkly green. She was living inside her stone, she thought.

Cinda loved pink: her hair turned pink, she always seemed to wear some sort of pink, and her room was pink. Pixie knew what Cinda's family stone was: the rose quartz.

Climbing up the ladder to help Tantra, Pixie had noticed Tantra's room was purple. Tantra always had purple shoelaces in her sneakers and purple wheels on her skateboard. Tantra's family stone had to be a purple one, maybe an amethyst.

Why were the stones important to find? Pixie started to wonder whether her mom knew about their family stone and that it was somewhere waiting to be found. Pixie hoped it wouldn't cause any problems like what they had experienced already.

Just then Pixie's mom entered the room and startled her out of her thoughts. "Pixie, how are you feeling? I noticed you didn't touch the soup at all. You really must not be feeling well today. That soup that your grandmother used to make is your favorite. Maybe you should stay home tomorrow, too."

"Mom, I think I just needed some sleep; I'm feeling much better. I am getting hungry now and that soup sounds good. I'd love to have some."

"Come on down. I think I'll join you in a bowl, too."

The two went down to the kitchen and sat quietly enjoying the meatball pasta soup that Grandma Josephine was famous for. Pixie needed to ask her mom about her family. Now was a better time than any.

"Mom, did Grandma ever talk about our family? Where we came from? Just anything?"

"I never really asked. Being the only child I was happy with my friends; they were my extended family. Why do you ask?"

"I just want to know more about Grandma. I miss her. We would always share great make-believe stories," said Pixie.

"I miss her too. She was very animated and loving; my mom meant everything to me." A tear fell down Mrs. Elm's cheek as Pixie got up to hug her.

"I love you, Mom."

"Hey, what's going on in here? Any love left for me?" asked Mr. Elm as he entered the kitchen, home from work.

"I love you too, Dad."

They all shared a group hug. "Do I see meatball soup? Oh, yes, I'll join in on that." Mr. Elm sat down to eat, sharing work stories and making Pixie and her mom laugh.

Pixie went to bed that night thinking about the next day and her search through the secret hallway to find her emerald stone. The last time she was in the hallway she noticed some moss growing on the walls. It seemed very odd to her then, but now that she had time to think about it everything seemed to make sense. The secret hallway was waiting for her all along, getting ready to present her with her emerald stone. Pixie fell into a deep sleep. A sleep she needed since finding the House of Charms.

Waking early to the sounds of her parents in the kitchen, Pixie jumped up, got ready, and ran down the steps in less than twenty minutes.

"Well, good morning. Someone seems like they're in a hurry this morning. What's going on in school that you're in a rush for?" asked Mr. Elm.

"It's the newspaper club; doesn't that start first thing in the morning?" asked Mrs. Elm.

Pixie had completely forgotten about the newspaper club, but she decided to use it as her excuse for being anxious to get to school. "Yes, it's the first day of our newspaper; I'm just excited to get started on it. I'm also looking forward to having less responsibility with it so I can focus on my own articles."

"I'm so proud of you, Pixie, to be so dedicated to a project that you love. This all benefits your future in college, you know," said Mr. Elm.

"I know, Dad."

Heading out to the bus stop earlier than normal, Pixie noticed that Cinda was already waiting. Her hair was down, with pink barrettes on the side, blond like it was before. Cinda turned around when she heard Pixie walking up behind her. "I guess that feather worked. Look at my hair; it's back to its normal color. I even think it's better then before. It seems to move so much more, don't you think?"

Cinda moved her head around to show Pixie how it swayed. She looked like she was acting for a shampoo commercial, Pixie thought. As long as Cinda was happy Pixie was fine watching her flicking her hair around.

"I'm so happy the pink is gone; I missed my blond hair. My mum seemed to be so relieved when she saw me this morning."

"You didn't tell her about the feather did you?" asked Pixie.

"No, are you crazy? She would want to know where I got an idea like that, and then I'd have to tell her. I'm sure she wouldn't be too happy knowing about our adventures."

"You're right about that," said Pixie.

Then Pixie told Cinda about the missing emerald and how she was going to try to find it that day in the secret hallway. She asked Cinda to go with her, but Cinda said she didn't want to because she was afraid that more strange things might happen to them. Pixie said she understood.

Walking into her homeroom after they'd arrived at school, Pixie noticed Carl already looking excited to start the newspaper. Joel was in his seat right behind Pixie's, talking with his friends and looking like he had been up to no good.

"Hey, Pixie. I've got some great ideas for the paper that I wanted to show you. What do you think about putting in a section where we ask students questions about their favorite things, like what bands they listen to or books they're reading, stuff like that?" asked Carl.

"That sounds great to me. We should pass it by Zeb first, but I have a feeling he'll think it's a good idea too."

"I still don't get this Zeb kid coming in and taking over your spot; you should be editor in chief, not him."

"Carl, I'm fine with it. Besides, I need a break this year. I have a lot going on in my life right now. I'll need the extra time to keep up with my schoolwork," Pixie said.

"If you say so," said Carl, who was quickly interrupted by Joel.

"What's this I hear? Is it true, Miss Special Pants Know It All didn't get picked to be editor in chief of the paper this year? Oh, boo-hoo, poor Pixie doesn't always get what she wants."

"Joel, mind your own business for once, will you?" Turning back around, Pixie gave him an evil look, one that she wished could hurt him. Not bad, but enough to make him stop picking on her.

As the bell rang, everyone got up to leave quickly, excited to start the club classes. Pixie and Carl walked through the crowds of people hanging out in the hallway. Pixie was on a mission to talk to Zeb before the newspaper club started. She had to tell him she needed time with homework and wouldn't be able to stay. That way she could sneak off to check out the hallway without anyone noticing. As Pixie and Carl arrived at the room, Pixie stopped outside the door.

"Hey, aren't you coming in?" asked Carl.

"I have to talk to Zeb first. I'll talk to you later," Pixie said. Carl looked at her strangely, feeling a little jealous that Pixie wanted to meet with Zeb alone.

Pixie waited for a while as the hallway started to clear. She got worried; maybe Zeb had changed his mind. Maybe he didn't want to be editor in chief after all, or maybe he decided to join Tantra in her club. This would mean Pixie would have to be in charge, which meant she wouldn't be able to leave for her search of the stone. Just then she heard someone running down the hallway, startling Pixie out of her thoughts. She looked up to see Zeb, his long hair swaying as he carried his books by his side.

"Hey, Pixie. Sorry I'm late. I had to talk to Mr. Zack about my woodworking project. Is something wrong? Why are you out in the hall?"

"I was waiting for you. I need a favor."

"Anything you want," said Zeb, smiling.

"I need to miss club this morning. I have to catch up on some homework. I hope you don't mind. I'll be able to make it to the rest of club classes, but just not today."

"I guess it's OK," said Zeb. "I was looking forward to working with you on this. I have some great ideas that I wanted to share with you."

"I'd love to hear them. I want to help out so bad today, but I'm falling behind in my classes. I just need to finish some assignments to catch up."

"Pixie, I don't want you to miss schoolwork; that's important. We can talk about it at lunch if you want."

"I would love that. I want to hear about everything that happens in club today. I'm so sorry to bail out like this on the first day; it's not like me to do this."

"I know it's not like you, I understand. Don't worry, we'll talk later."

Zeb gave her a hug and then entered the club where everyone started calling out to him: "Hey, Zeb, how's it going?" "What should we do?" Pixie listened, wishing she could join in, but she really needed to get to the secret hallway soon; she needed all the time she could get.

Pixie took off down the hall to a side door of the auditorium. Opening the door she forgot that some students opted for study hall instead of a club and the auditorium was occupied. In fact, it was packed. How was she supposed to just walk in without anyone noticing and open the door inside the stage to the secret hallway? It seemed impossible until she noticed something very odd. The auditorium was completely silent; everyone had their eyes closed, even the teachers. How strange, Pixie thought. Could they be under a spell? Was it her emerald stone wanting to be found like Lillian had said? Or had Lillian caused this herself?

Pixie walked to the door and casually opened it. She went down the stairs, noticing mounds of grass and blossoms growing on the steps leading to what used to be the secret hallway. She now found herself walking in a forest with beautiful tall trees, green grass, flowers of every kind and large mushrooms surrounding what seemed to be a lake up ahead. Birds were chirping while a slight breeze ruffled the air. It was dark, but just light enough for her to see a path made of gold sparkly dust illuminating her every step. You're not at Cedar High anymore, Pixie thought.

She decided to follow the sparkly trail. Everywhere she turned there was something beautiful to see. Birds were flying through the large trees, while butterflies chased each other around her head. Moss covered the ground completely, and large mushrooms grew in bunches scattered throughout the forest.

Everything seemed to have a breathing life of its own. Pixie walked slowly on the trail, not wanting to walk too fast and miss finding her stone. What did it look like? Was it small or large? She knew it was an emerald; Lillian had told her that much at least. As she continued walking she noticed some deer running up ahead, but she couldn't see where they were going.

The sounds of crickets and frogs filled the air. Every once in a while Pixie would see a frog or two jumping from one mushroom to another. Lightning bugs flitted in the sky like twinkling stars. Everything was so beautiful, and for some reason Pixie felt right at home in this forest. An owl from out of nowhere flew in front of her face, making her jump. She heard rustling from the bushes up ahead. Frightened that she may have startled a wild animal, Pixie stayed very still until whatever was in the bushes decided to leave. Then she caught a glimpse of two squirrels running out from underneath the bushes. They looked up at her briefly and then took off down the sparkly trail. One of them seemed to have an acorn in its paws, and the other one was holding something green and shiny. Pixie followed the squirrel, trying to get a better look at what it had tucked under its arm. As she got closer, she shouted loudly, "Oh, my, the emerald stone!"

The squirrels took off. The one with the stone stuck it in his cheek and chased the other squirrel deep into the woods, off the glittery trail.

Pixie chased them, jumping over sticks and logs and pushing away bushes. She ran in complete darkness with only the green glow from the squirrel's cheek to help guide her. They came upon a brook, which the squirrels jumped over. Pixie followed close behind, slipping on the wet rocks as she tried to catch up.

"Hey, you squirrels slow down; I need that stone." The squirrels slid under a branch and Pixie decided to jump over it. But she underestimated its height and, to her dismay, she tripped, landing right on top of the squirrel with the stone in his cheek.

The emerald popped out of the squirrel's mouth as he squeezed out from under her and ran after the other squirrel, leaving the stone behind.

The emerald stone was three inches away from Pixie's head, but unable to move after her fall, she had no idea it was right there. Pixie fell into a dreamlike state, completely forgetting where she was or why she was there. Everything seemed very dark around her as she lapsed into a comatose sleep.

Suddenly a bright light came from the woods up ahead; Pixie opened her eyes just in time to notice it shining on her. Slowly trying to lift herself up, she heard a familiar voice. It was very comforting and loving, and she realized it was Holly Hawthorn, the school nurse. She was wearing her nurse's uniform, which glowed and seemed to be the source of the white light.

Pixie looked up at Holly. "Miss Hawthorn, hi; it's me, Pixie. I seem to have lost my way."

"Well, of course, my dear. I'm here to help. Come take my hand; I know the way." As Pixie grabbed Miss Hawthorn's hand, the landscape radiated beautiful colors, almost like walking through a painting. She could hear her footsteps so clear and pronounced, and she could taste all the colors.

Pixie laughed. "Where are we, Miss Hawthorn?"

"Pixie? Pixie, wake up. Your mom is here to take you home." Pixie opened her eyes and stared into Holly Hawthorn's above her. Startled to find herself in the nurse's office, she jumped out of bed.

"Wait a minute; what just happened? How did we get here? I don't remember any of this."

"Pixie, I think you must have come down with something. I found you sleeping in the hallway," said Miss Hawthorn.

"But I was in a forest trying to find something. I left school somehow. I don't remember now. I'm not going crazy, am I?"

"Oh, no, Pixie, you're fine. I just think you should take another day off; you need it," said Holly, whispering in Pixie's ear.

Mrs. Elm walked in looking worried. "Pixie, what happened? Are you all right? Holly called and said she found you sleeping in the hallway. I knew you weren't getting enough sleep. What am I going to do with you?"

"Mom, I'm fine. I'll try to get more sleep."

"Alright, we have an agreement. Thanks so much, Holly, for taking care of her. I told Dana that we ran into each other and she wants to get together this weekend. How does that sound?"

"That would be great. Let me know what time and I'll be there," said Holly.

"Alright, Pixie, let's go."

"Bye, Miss Hawthorn. Thanks for everything," Pixie said.

"Oh, it was nothing," said Holly, laughing. "Pixie, don't forget your dreams; they are powerful, you know." Holly smiled at Pixie.

"I won't," said Pixie with a perplexed look.

On the ride home from school Pixie's mom lectured her about the importance of getting the proper amount of sleep. As her mom talked, Pixie stared out the window, trying to remember what had happened to her. She seemed to have lost her memory for that brief time right before she woke in the nurse's office.

Something was coming back to her; she remembered searching for something. Then she started to remember everything little by little: the forest with the sparkly path, the butterflies, the mushrooms and those two squirrels. She had chased them for some reason, but why? Then she remembered why: the emerald stone. That's it! They had the stone. She then remembered falling and waking to a beautiful glow of white light. It was Holly. She was there; she knows about the secret hallway.

"Oh, no! Mom, I need to go back to school. I forgot to get something, it's real important."

"Pixie, we're almost home. What did you forget? Why don't we call the school and have Cinda bring it home for you."

Pixie reluctantly decided to agree with her mom. There was always next week to look for the emerald. "Hopefully those squirrels don't have it again," Pixie thought out loud.

"What did you say?" asked Pixie's mom as they pulled into the driveway.

"Nothing. I was just thinking about something I read in English class, that's all." That was close, thought Pixie to herself.

Pixie followed her mom into the house and headed up to her room.

"I'll wake you for lunch," called Mrs. Elm.

"Thanks, Mom. That sounds good."

Pixie was starting to feel a little tired, probably from all the exploring she did in the forest that morning. She dropped her backpack on the floor and lay down for a while. She thought about the forest and Holly being there to help. Why didn't Holly tell her mom that she had found her in the forest instead of saying she fell asleep in the hallway? Was Holly trying to cover for her, knowing that her mom might be upset with Pixie if she knew the truth?

As Pixie lay on her bed, she put her hands in her pockets and touched something deep in her left jeans pocket. She slowly lifted it up to the light from her window. Pixie stared at it in total shock. How could it be? She was holding up the emerald stone. The stone was a perfect oval shape and filled the room with a green glow.

She could now go back to the House of Charms with the stone. Everything was falling into place; it was all happening. What it was, though, she did not know.

Chapter 13

The Green Dress

The morning sun shone through Pixie's bedroom window on the crisp Saturday morning as she stretched and woke up in anticipation of taking the stone back to Lillian. She wanted to find out the truth about her family.

"You're up early again," said Mrs. Elm as Pixie strolled downstairs for breakfast. "Don't you think you should rest a little longer? I've never heard of someone so tired that they fall asleep in a hallway."

"She looks fine. Good morning, Sunshine. How are things? School going good?" Mr. Elm asked.

"Yes, Dad. Everything is going fine. I feel great today. I'm going to call Cinda this morning to see if she's interested in a nature walk; it's for another project for school," Pixie lied.

"Today is definitely a great day for a walk -- the sky is blue, the air crisp and the leaves are changing colors. I love this time of year," said Mr. Elm.

"Do you remember that time last year when we took a walk in the woods on a day just like today and all of a sudden the sky darkened and the rain came down in buckets? The three of us ran like crazy back to the house completely drenched. That was fun," said Pixie's mom, laughing.

"Yes, it was," Pixie's dad said.

"Holly is coming over this afternoon. I want you to stop in sometime around one to say hello," Mrs. Elm said.

"I will. I hope I can finish my project early today; I'm not sure how long it will take," said Pixie.

"Holly is so nice. I haven't seen her in years," said Mrs. Elm.

"That's odd that she hasn't popped around here earlier since her brother lives next door," said Mr. Elm. His wife shot him a look.

"Holly's brother lives next door? Who's her brother?" asked Pixie.

"Well, they're not that close so I'm not surprised that she's never stopped for a visit," Mrs. Elm said.

"Tantra's father is Holly's brother," said Mr. Elm.

"Why don't they get along? Holly seems so nice; I can't see her not getting along with anyone," said Pixie.

"I guess it's just some childhood thing that has gone on for a while," said Pixie's father. "Maybe this visit will be a start of new beginnings. You never know what may happen in life."

"That is definitely true," said Pixie. "I'm going to give Cinda a call to see if she can meet me outside so we can get started early."

"Alright, just remember to try to make it back around one o'clock," said Mrs. Elm.

"No problem," Pixie said as she headed out the back door. While calling Cinda she held her emerald up to the sky to catch the light.

"Good morning, I was wondering what you're up to this morning," Pixie said when Cinda answered.

"Pixie, what happened to you yesterday? I heard rumors that you passed out and had to be carried to the nurse's office. Is that true?"

"I'm not sure. All I remember is going to the secret hallway that I told you about, and when I got there it changed into a forest. The next thing I knew, the nurse was looking down at me in her office."

"Pixie, I think it's that woman Lillian; she's putting spells on us. It's dangerous to continue this whole thing. I wish you would end it now."

"I can't. I found the emerald stone."

"You found the stone? Where? You just said you don't remember anything."

"I found it in the forest," Pixie said. "I remember being there, just not how I got out."

"I suppose you're going back there today with that stone," Cinda said. "And I'm also guessing that you think I may want to go with you this time. Am I right?"

"Well, yes, I was hoping you would," Pixie said.

"I don't want to; I'm sorry," Cinda said.

"Cinda, please, I think this is it. Don't you want to know what it all means?"

"Not particularly."

"Alright," Pixie said, "if not for that then how about for Noon? It may be my last trip out there. I have a feeling you would never go there by yourself."

"He did draw me that picture," Cinda said. "He's so nice, not like most of the boys in school. I would like to see him again."

"I'm outside. Meet me by the oak tree when you're ready," Pixie said. "Hurry up; I want to leave soon."

"OK, I'll be right there."

Pixie hung up and sat on the back porch for a minute before heading over to the oak tree to wait for Cinda. While she waited she could hear her parents talking in the kitchen.

"I wish you didn't bring up the subject of Holly and Tovey being brother and sister," Mrs. Elm said.

"What's the big deal? Pixie doesn't know anything about all that; all she knows is that they haven't seen each other for years," said Mr. Elm.

"Well, everything is tied into that night. I just feel somewhat responsible," said Mrs. Elm.

"You all did what you thought was right. There's nothing wrong with that," Mr. Elm told his wife.

"Are you ready? You look lost right now," asked Cinda as she approached Pixie by the tree.

"Oh, I guess I was in a fog for a moment. I'm ready now; let's go," Pixie said as Cinda followed her into the forest. "I wonder what Lillian will tell us now that I've found the stone."

"She freaks me out. That whole pink hair thing was enough for me, but you obviously like to be tortured," said Cinda.

"Oh, stop. No one is getting tortured."

"Wait a second; is that Tantra up ahead?" Cinda asked.

"I think so. It's odd to see her alone like that."

The girls walked up to the bridge where Tantra was sitting, and as they got closer they noticed she had a sketch pad with her and was drawing a picture of a tree.

"Hey, funny seeing you here. What are you doing by yourself?" asked Pixie.

"For your information I happen to like being by myself once in a while. I come out here to get away from people like you," Tantra said.

"Oh, Tantra, you don't need to act tough all the time," Cinda said. "We are neighbors, you know, why not make an effort to be nice?"

"You're asking for the impossible," Pixie said.

"Whatever. Why don't the two of you just continue going on your merry way," Tantra said.

Cinda sat down next to Tantra and looked at her sketch pad. "You're really good. I didn't know you liked to draw," she said.

"You don't need to sit down next to me. Take off now, please."

"We're sorry; it's just odd to see you out here," Cinda said.

"Well, I like it out here. It feels nice, makes me feel good. Why are you two out here? Not that I really care or anything," Tantra said.

"We're heading to the House of Charms," Pixie said. "I found an emerald stone that Lillian wanted me to find. She said she would let us know about the things I found in my grandmother's trunk. Why don't you come along? This could be the last trip."

"No, thanks. I've had enough fun with the two of you. I don't need to revisit all of that again," Tantra said.

"Suit yourself," said. Pixie. "Come on, Cinda. Let's go."

Cinda got up and followed Pixie deeper into the woods. Tantra watched them go until she couldn't see them anymore, then continued her drawing.

The two girls finally approached the dead part of the forest, and as soon as they entered they started to feel different.

"Pixie, do you feel anything right now?" Cinda asked.

"I was just going to ask you the same thing."

"I feel so happy, my whole body has goose bumps. I feel like laughing and dancing right now, what about you?"

"Me too," said Pixie.

They ran through with their arms outstretched, laughing and skipping. As they approached the end of the dead area they slowed down, trying to find their way through the high brush that covered the trail to the House of Charms.

Looking down at the ground for the trail, they came to the clearing where the large boulders were. "This is it; it's right up here," said Pixie.

The two girls stood in front of the old shack and stared at the crooked sign hanging above the door. They walked up and knocked. Just like the times before, the door mysteriously opened by itself.

They walked in, surrounded by all the offerings in the front store. The butterflies and lightning bugs flew around their heads, while the bees occupied themselves around the flowers in the corner of the shop. Everything seemed to be perfectly normal to Pixie.

"Hello, Lillian? Noon? Is anyone here? It's Pixie and Cinda; we've come back with the emerald stone." A rustling sound started in the corner of the shop, like someone was crunching up newspaper. "Hello, is anyone there?"

The back door opened, making whatever was in the corner scurry across the floor in front of them. Cinda let out a scream. "What was that?"

The footsteps from the back door moved toward the front of the house. "Is everything alright? What happened?"

There standing in front of Cinda was Noon, his long, dark hair tosseled, his clothes slightly dirty. "Cinda, are you alright?" he asked as he approached her with a hug.

"I'm fine. Something ran across the floor and we were startled," said Cinda, gazing into Noon's eyes.

"It's great to see you again," said Noon.

"Same here," said Cinda, looking down bashfully.

"Look, there it is again," said Pixie.

A small animal ran across the floor toward Noon and grabbed his leg. Noon reached down and picked it up. "This little guy is a hedgehog. I named him Tink because he is always tinkering around; he's harmless. He likes to run around exploring. I found him out back. He looked lost so I decided to take him in until he could find his way home. How do you like the vest I made for him?"

Cinda and Pixie walked up to pet Tink. "He's so cute. I've never heard of a hedgehog living in this area before," said Cinda. Pixie rubbed Tink's ears, making him giggle.

"He's my buddy," said Noon. "It's so great to see both of you again; can you stay for a while?"

"I'd love to," said Cinda.

"Great. I'll make us some tea. Which would you like, mint or jasmine?"

"I'll have mint, thanks," said Cinda.

"Me too, please," said Pixie before leaning over to whisper to her friend. "Cinda, we're here to talk to Lillian, and don't forget I have to be back by one."

"I know, I know," Cinda said.

"Alright, you hang with Noon while I talk to Lillian," said Pixie.

Noon came back and said: "Come into the kitchen; we can hang out there."

The girls followed him into the kitchen, which was definitely not ordinary. Along one wall was a purple

157

couch with a coffee table made from trees, no doubt something Noon had built. The cabinets were filled with herbs and vegetables. The stove looked very old. A few homemade utensils were on the table. Noon lit a candle and put it on the coffee table, giving the room a nice glow.

"Noon, is Lillian here? I found the emerald stone she wanted me to get the last time I came to visit."

"You did! Yes, she is here. She will be happy to hear that," Noon said. "I could take you up to the library; she's up there."

"That would be great." Pixie got up to follow Noon while Cinda stayed behind.

Lillian, dressed in her purple dress and red robe, seemed to have aged quite a bit from the last visit. She was reading one of the large books on her old wooden table. She looked up slowly at Pixie. "Ah, you're back. I could tell that you found the stone; I felt it. I'm an old woman starting to get weaker with each new discovery you make. We're on track. Have a seat, and let me see this stone."

Pixie walked over to the table and sat across from Lillian. "I'll be downstairs if you need me," said Noon as he left quickly.

Pixie pulled out the stone and placed it on the table. "Aahh, the stone," Lillian said as she picked it up slowly and turned it in all directions to catch the light. The emerald filled the room with a green glow. Lillian reached her hand to her neck, pulling a necklace out from under her purple dress. The necklace had a large ruby in the center with four empty spots around it. As Lillian held the necklace in one hand and the emerald with the other, she let the stone go. It magically snapped into place at the top empty spot on the necklace right above the ruby, leaving three empty spots.

"This is good, Pixie. You found your stone; you'll grow so much into who you are now."

"Lillian, you said that if I found the stone you would tell me more about my grandmother's things and what they all mean."

"Yes, I did. I will tell you this: Those dreams you had were real; there was a fire that killed many. Some of your ancestors died that day. They died because they weren't accepted in society because they were unique. Only three young girls survived that day, and I took them in. One of them was an Elm, the other a Willow, and the third a Birch. Now all three families live side by side again. There is no fighting what your families have tried to hide for a long time now. It is time for the three of you girls to claim your heritage. Don't be afraid of who you are."

"Who are we?" asked Pixie.

"That's all the information I can only give you for now, unfortunately. There is a dress you must find; each one of you girls has a dress somewhere out there. These dresses have been handed down for generations secretly, but I'm afraid that for safety's sake some of them could have been destroyed."

"Lillian, I have that dress," Pixie said.

Lillian stood up, knocking over her stool. "Child, you cannot be serious."

"It's in my grandmother's trunk," Pixie said. "It has to be the dress you're talking about."

"Pixie, you must go home right now and bring it here at once. You will know all and be all. Go. Go now."

"I will. I just have one question: How could you still be alive if you were the one in my dreams? Didn't that happen sometime in the 1800s?"

"I'll tell you about that later," Lillian said. "You will know one day when all the dresses have been found. Please, child, go now; bring the dress back."

Pixie ran down the stairs calling to Cinda. "Cinda! Cinda we have to go now. I need to get that green dress from my grandmother's trunk." Pixie entered the kitchen, catching Noon and Cinda in a long kiss. "Excuse me for interrupting," she said.

Noon pulled away, still looking at Cinda, who said, "I, I'm sorry, we were just..."

"I know, just kissing. That's fine," Pixie said. "Cinda, we have to go. I have to go get the dress; we'll be right back."

"OK, we'll go," said Cinda, slowly getting up from the couch and staring at Noon.

"Cinda, please," said Pixie as she grabbed her arm and dragged her out.

Noon pushed his hair out of his face as he followed them. "I'll see both of you later. Cinda, I want you to have something – wait." Noon handed Cinda a necklace made of braided leather with a handcrafted metal heart pendant. He had taken it from around his neck and placed it around Cinda's.

"I couldn't, Noon; it's yours."

"No, please. I want you to have it."

"Thanks. It's beautiful." Cinda held the heart in her hands as she looked up at Noon.

"You girls better go; I'll see you soon." Noon kissed Cinda on the forehead before he walked back into the house with Tink following.

Pixie and Cinda started running through the woods back home. "Pixie, what happened?" Cinda said. "Why do you need the dress?"

"It's the last thing I need to do. It represents our heritage, something our parents are afraid of because we're different from other people," Pixie said.

"What is it? Why are we different?" asked Cinda, trying to catch up to Pixie.

"We will know once I get that dress."

As they came to the clearing Pixie spotted something moving. "Wait, look. Isn't that your grandfather over there?" she asked.

"Why would my grandfather be out in these woods? That's ridiculous." Cinda leaned over and looked where Pixie was pointing. "It *is* him! What is he doing?"

The girls walked over to Cinda's grandfather, who seemed to be collecting old pieces of wood and putting them inside a large sack.

"Grandpa, what are you doing?"

"Hey, girls. It's so nice to see the both of you out here. It's such a lovely place, don't you think?"

"Grandpa, everything is dead here. How can it be lovely?"

"It was once," said Pixie, looking at Cinda's grandpa.

"That's right, Pixie. It was and will be again. You girls continue on. Go on now. It's happening, you know; it's happening."

"What's happening, Grandpa?" asked Cinda.

"Come on, let's go. I have a feeling he knows what we're up to," Pixie said.

"This is so weird," Cinda said. "See you, Grandpa."

"Bye, my sweet granddaughter. I knew you would be the one."

The girls got closer to the bridge and noticed that Tantra was still there. She was lying down with her iPod on. Pixie and Cinda ran past, waking her up. "Hey, what's wrong with you two? I was sleeping here; don't interrupt me like that."

"We need to get a dress. Pixie is going to find out what our heritage is. We're going back," said Cinda as she ran to keep up with Pixie.

As the girls entered the back door of Pixie's house, voices could be heard from the living room. "Pixie, is that you? Come here and say hello to Holly," called Mrs. Elm.

"Come on, let's just say hi, hang for a few minutes and then take off," said Pixie.

"Sounds great," said Cinda.

"Hello, girls. Nice to see you both. Hanging out in the woods, I hear," said Holly as she looked at them with a smile.

"Yes, we're working on a school project," said Pixie.

"Dana, Cinda looks so much like you," Holly said.

"Oh, to be young again," Dana said, and the three women laughed.

"Pixie, guess what? Holly ran into Mr. Bloom the other day. She has his new number; wouldn't it be fun to start those harp lessons again?" asked Mrs. Elm.

"That would be great, Mom. It's been awhile since I played," Pixie said.

"Cinda and I need to go back out to collect some more things, and I need to get my backpack so we have something to put them in," Pixie said.

"Alright, you two. I'm glad you're working on your homework on a Saturday afternoon," said Mrs. Willow.

"Don't stay out too late; I heard we may get a storm coming in soon," said Mrs. Elm.

"We won't," said Cinda as she followed Pixie upstairs to her room.

"The key is under the floorboard in my closet," said Pixie. She lifted up the floorboard and reached in, feeling around.

"Well, where is it?" asked Cinda.

"I don't know; it's not here anymore. I know I put it back. Where could it be? I don't get it."

"Let's go up to your attic. Maybe by chance the trunk is open," said Cinda.

"Maybe, but I doubt it," said Pixie, clearly upset.

As the girls left Pixie's room they bumped into Holly in the hallway. "Sorry, girls. I didn't mean to startle you. Oh, Popixopie, three times a charm," said Holly, smiling at them as she headed to the bathroom.

"What does that mean?" asked Cinda, looking at Pixie.

"That means Holly knows how to speak Opish; she said my name in Op language. I think she was trying to help us out somehow, and I think I know how. Come on, let's get up to the attic quick before our moms come upstairs."

"Here's the trunk; just what I thought," Pixie said when they reached the attic. "It's locked and there's no key in sight."

"What should we do now?" Cinda said.

"Holly said my name in Opish and then said, 'three times a charm.' I wonder if the charm is for me to say my grandmother's name three times in Opish."

"Try it," said Cinda.

Pixie put her hands on the trunk and said her grandmother's name in Opish three times: "Joposopephinope Opelm." The trunk opened with a click.

"I don't believe it; it worked," said Cinda.

Pixie lifted the lid and moved the books and papers aside so she could get the dress out. She put it up to her body, noticing it was the perfect size.

"Pixie, that dress was made for you, even if it's a little old-fashioned. What is that hanging from it?" Cinda said.

"I'm not sure; it looks like sand, green sand," said Pixie.

"Put it in your backpack and let's go," said Cinda. Pixie did so and closed the trunk, which locked by itself.

163

They headed out of the attic and down the stairs to the kitchen, where Mrs. Elm, Mrs. Willow and Holly now were.

"Don't be too long, girls," said Mrs. Elm.

"Bye, girls. I hope you get what you're looking for," said Holly, smiling.

"We will. Thanks, Holly," said Pixie, smiling back.

Cinda and Pixie ran to the woods through Pixie's backyard. They got to the bridge where Tantra was still hanging out, listening to her music and drawing. Tantra looked up. "Are you two for real; you're really going back there? Cinda, I didn't expect you to be so into this with the pink hair thing and all."

"Yeah, well, Noon's there, and Pixie is going to find out more about us. Don't you want to know about your heritage?" asked Cinda.

"I know it already. I'm a mix of Spanish and Asian; that's all I need to know," Tantra said.

"When we find out what else, we'll let you know if you're interested," said Pixie.

Pixie and Cinda took off again through the woods back to the House of Charms. Tantra watched and this time decided to follow. She walked just enough behind so they didn't know she was there.

Making good time, the girls reached the boulder and stopped. "This is it now; I'm a little afraid of what we may find out. I hope it's nothing bad," said Pixie.

"Pixie, I've been thinking about that too, and I don't think it will be bad. All of these things are from your grandmother, someone you loved. And she would never try to harm you. I really do believe that the trunk was left for you. She wanted you to find it because she knew how adventurous you are and that you would be the one to make a change. I say go for it; I'm right here with you."

"Thanks, Cinda."

The two girls hugged as Tantra watched, overhearing everything.

Pixie and Cinda walked to the front door. They could smell a fire burning in the fireplace; Noon must have started it. Cinda knocked on the door. Instead of it opening by itself, Lillian opened the door and let the girls in. "Oh, Cinda, it is so good to see you too. I'm glad you decided to join Pixie today on this very special occasion."

"Thanks, Lillian," said Cinda as she looked at Lillian's necklace with the ruby and emerald in place, noticing the three missing stones.

"Come on upstairs to the library; we will do this up there." Lillian slowly closed the door, staring outside as if feeling a presence nearby. She led the girls up the stairs to the library. The table was moved to the side and a platform was now in the center of the room.

"The dress, where is the dress?" asked Lillian. Pixie took off her backpack and unzipped it, pulling out the dress carefully. "It is, it is the dress," said Lillian excitedly . "Pixie please put it on; you can change behind the bookcase. Then come out and stand on the platform."

Pixie did as she was told while Lillian and Cinda waited by the platform. "Where is Noon?" Cinda asked Lillian. "I sent him out; he is not ready to know about this yet. I must say, dear, he was quite upset to leave. He has quite a liking for you."

Cinda blushed. "I have quite a liking for him too." Lillian smiled at Cinda.

Pixie walked out from behind the bookcase and stood on the platform. Both Cinda and Lillian looked surprised. "What's wrong? Is everything alright? Does it fit me? I feel a little silly; it's really not my style."

The dress started to illuminate; it sparkled green and brightened the whole room. The bag of dust attached to the dress seemed to find a life of its own, breathing in and out with powerful sparkly green glitter radiating from it. The sight was overwhelming.

"Pixie, you're beautiful; you look like an angel," said Cinda.

"I feel different, in a good way," said Pixie.

"You, Pixie Elm, have now brought your heritage line back to life. You can do many things now. You will learn over time what gifts you have and their benefits. Use them wisely. They're not magic, although it may seem like it. You can never go back, only forward. You have changed right before our eyes. Others will sense the change but will not guess what it is."

"What am I?" asked Pixie.

"You're a Woodland Faerie," Lillian said. "Your ancestors were Woodland Faeries. When they were found out, most were killed. Three survived from this group: an Elm, a Willow and a Birch.

"This is just the beginning; the rest of the changes cannot happen until all is found. If you noticed my necklace, it's still missing three stones. They need to be found by their owners.

Once they are all found, the Woodland Faeries will live again in this area. All will accept them. The heritage will last forever, with no need to hide from fear. We will be proud of who we are."

"Lillian you mentioned three more stones; is one of those mine?" asked Cinda.

Lillian turned and looked at Cinda. She seemed to have aged even more from the last time Cinda had looked at her. "Yes, my child. Your stone is out there waiting for you. I guess you also know you have a dress to find as well."

"I'm not sure my mom kept our dress. I'm not even sure where to look," said Cinda.

"I know where your dress is," said Pixie.

"You do? Where?"

"It's in England. That's why your mom went back; she went there to find the dress. That's probably why she came back disappointed, because she didn't find it."

"Of course she didn't find it, it's not meant for her to find anymore. It's your dress, Cinda; you're the one who needs to find it," said Lillian.

"Pixie, we need to go to England. How and when? Our parents will never let us go," said Cinda.

"Things have changed, you will see," Lillian said. "You will find a way. The green dress has been brought back to life; the pink dress will want its life back too."

"Did you say pink? Pink is my favorite color; how great is that?" laughed Cinda.

"That's good because before you search for your dress you will need to find your stone, the rose quartz, which is also pink, and I have a feeling it is somewhere here in New York. I haven't picked up its location yet; I will let you know when I do," Lillian told Cinda.

"Pixie, you'll help me, won't you?" asked Cinda.

"Of course I will."

"It's happening, girls. I would keep this to yourselves for now. I have a feeling your parents are not ready for this yet. They need a push, which we'll give them when everything is found," said Lillian.

Leaning against the house just below the library window, Tantra had heard all of it. She even saw the green light shine through the window and send sparkles in the air. She heard the unbelievable story: Pixie was a Woodland Faerie, so was Cinda and so was she. Tantra decided to walk back home to try to make sense of it all. As she started to turn back, she ran into Noon who was walking to the House of Charms.

"Hey, how are you? You look upset about something. Is everything alright?" asked Noon.

"I'm not sure what I am. I just need to be alone," said Tantra, who had a tear in her eye. Noon watched her walk away.

Tantra had noticed a mark on Noon's neck that looked like a half moon. She was going to bring it up to him but decided to walk back to her house instead. She continued to listen to her music, something that made her feel good no matter what was going on in her life at the time: What better song than her favorite, "Trees."

Back at the House of Charms, Pixie changed into her regular clothes and put the dress back into her backpack. It returned to its natural green color, but the bag kept sparkling and shining brightly: her heritage, for the whole world to see. She was proud of who she was and loved her grandmother for showing her the way.

"Girls, once the rose quartz and the pink dress have been found, Cinda will become a Woodland Faerie too."

"I can't believe it, Pixie; we're Woodland Fairies," said Cinda.

"I never would have guessed. I thought that was just all make believe," said Pixie.

"You can always come to visit anytime you like. We would love to have your company," said Lillian.

"We will," said Pixie.

"I feel like we are family now," said Cinda.

"We are; the sooner you find your dress the stronger our family will be," said Lillian.

"Let us know when and where to search for the rose quartz. We'll start right away," said Pixie.

"Tell Noon I said hi and that I will visit soon," said Cinda.

"I will, dear, and as soon as I get a feel for your stone I will let you know," said Lillian.

The girls left the House of Charms, running through the woods happy and in good spirits. "Look, it's Noon up ahead," said Pixie.

"It is Noon! Hey, over here," called Cinda.

Noon looked up with a smile as he ran over to them. "Cinda, Pixie, I thought I wouldn't get the chance to see you again today," he said.

Cinda hugged Noon. "I hope it's OK if I come out to visit every once in a while," said Cinda.

"OK? Are you kidding -- that would be great," Noon said.

"We have to get home before our parents start to worry about us, but don't forget, I'll be back," said Cinda.

"I won't," said Noon. "The two of you look like you're happy; I guess it was a positive outcome, then?" asked Noon.

"Yes, it was," said Pixie.

"I was worried when I saw Tantra upset, I thought something bad had happened," said Noon.

"You saw Tantra? Where was she?" asked Cinda.

"She was walking away from the House of Charms; I thought she was with the two of you."

"She knows," said Pixie to Cinda.

"Knows what?" asked Noon.

"Oh, nothing to worry about. We'll let you know when we can."

"You better. I'll let you two go home now; it's starting to get dark," said Noon as he hugged Pixie and Cinda, giving Cinda a kiss on her forehead. "Don't forget me out here."

"We won't, don't worry," said Cinda, smiling back at him.

The sky started to darken and rain soon began to drop down hard. It was one of those strange nights on Cedar Wood Way, a night when the rain mixed with the fog, making it hard to see. Both Cinda and Pixie were completely soaked as they made it through the woods, laughing, neither one minding the rain.

They held hands as they arrived at Pixie's backyard and spun each other around. "I'll see you tomorrow, Pixie," said Cinda as she hugged her friend.

"Yes," said Pixie, and they both took off to their houses.

Pixie ran up the porch and opened the back door, her hair plastered to her face. "I'm home," she called out. "I've come home." Looking down at herself, she suddenly noticed that she was completely dry; even her hair had become dry all by itself. Must be one of the many perks of becoming a Woodland Faerie, Pixie thought to herself as she walked happily into her home.

Coming Soon

About the Author

Christina Cameron

Growing up in a small town in New York has always been an inspiration for her creative soul. Surrounded by a thick forest area and living with nature's beautiful changes of the season's will always be a part of her spirit. Living in California has also added a whole new wonderful taste of life experiences.

40243796R00111

Made in the USA
Charleston, SC
31 March 2015